The November Deep

Elizabeth Woodworth

SALAMANCA PRESS
Victoria, Canada

Salamanca Press
3909 Persimmon Drive
Victoria, British Colombia
Canada
V8P 3R8

tel. (250) 383-2417

Canadian Cataloguing in Publication Data

Woodworth, Elizabeth, 1943-
    The November deep

    ISBN 1-55212-579-3

    I. Title.
PS8595.O6596N68 2001   C813'.6   C00-911516-1
PR9199.3.W642N68 2001

TRAFFORD

This book was published *on-demand* in cooperation with Trafford Publishing.
On-demand publishing is a unique process and service of making a book available for retail sale to the public taking advantage of on-demand manufacturing and Internet marketing.
On-demand publishing includes promotions, retail sales, manufacturing, order fulfilment, accounting and collecting royalties on behalf of the author.

Suite 6E, 2333 Government St., Victoria, B.C. V8T 4P4, CANADA

Phone	250-383-6864	Toll-free	1-888-232-4444 (Canada & US)
Fax	250-383-6804	E-mail	sales@trafford.com
Web site	www.trafford.com	TRAFFORD PUBLISHING IS A DIVISION OF TRAFFORD HOLDINGS LTD.	
Trafford Catalogue #00-0245		www.trafford.com/robots/00-0245.html	

10   9   8   7   6   5   4   3   2

Dedication

To those who decide that there is choice, and work to
make themselves whole;
And to those who don't, and thus endure
The full limitations of their fate.
To those who use the tool of choice to rise above their
lesser selves.
To those who choose hopefulness over cynicism.
To those who choose to imagine a better world, and then
strive to create it.
And to those who invite the beauty of silent mind.
When the good is chosen, delight enters the moment;
Followed by gratitude, compassion, and love.

Acknowledgements

I would like to acknowledge the teachings of Jiddu
Krishnamurti (1895-1986), who sought to free human
intelligence from the bonds of authority – both outside the
self and within it.

And I acknowledge the spirit of Mother Teresa (1910-
1997), who used this short prayer as her "business card".
It is psychic architecture at its best.

> *"The fruit of silence is prayer;*
> *The fruit of prayer is faith;*
> *The fruit of faith is love;*
> *The fruit of love is service;*
> *The fruit of service is peace."*

Here at home, I am especially grateful to my husband
Claud for his support and patience during the many days
when I was fully absorbed in writing.

Elizabeth Woodworth
January, 2001

CHAPTER 1

Nell Fitzgerald O'Donovan slept fitfully. With each gust the roaring northeaster pounded the old Minto dinghy against the side of the house. Nell, having flown in late from Toronto, was too tired to rouse herself and sandwiched her head between the pillows. Throughout the night storm, sheets of rain rattled the windows and thunder cracked like rifle-fire over the dark ocean. Finally there came silence, and with it deep sleep.

Nell awakened. The far but distinct drone of a small plane conjured up the image of a clear blue sky. When she rose to draw the curtains light streamed into the room and the bay beyond sparkled in the November sun.

She returned to the big double bed with its view over Georgia Strait, yawned, and stretched luxuriously against the crisp cotton sheets. The airplane engine was growing steadily louder, and a familiar sorrow gripped her as a light floatplane descended past the window for a landing across the bay.

It had been a full year since Patrick had dropped his helicopter onto a mountainside during the last leg of a rescue operation. She'd had a fleeting premonition that morning as his tweed back disappeared through the front door that she might never see him again. The search and rescue people had called late in the evening; Patrick had ferried several loads of shivering children from the mountain ledge before taking off for the last group. In the fading light a snowstorm had engulfed the helicopter as it descended into the small forest clearing at the foot of the cliff.

One of the rotors had hit a tree, and Patrick had been killed instantly as the machine spun into the rock face. Lovely, old-soul Patrick, with his Irish lisp, curly black hair, and merry eyes -- how had death been possible?

For months the vision of Patrick's death would stop Nell's breath and produce a stillness in the region of her heart, but on this sunny morning she tossed back the covers to throw off the mood, and headed downstairs for the coffee pot.

Though her anguish over Patrick had burned down to embers, he continued in some way to reside within her. She had internalized him even before his death, and would often consult him on a point of judgement or share a moment of humour with him. Life with anyone else still seemed out of the question. She had no problem being alone in any case; the problem was loneliness for Patrick, with whom she had felt completely at home on all levels of her being.

Today was Thursday and a free day. Nell opened the French doors and stepped out of the kitchen onto the ground-level balcony, strolling around to inspect the festive array of colours. Waiting for the kettle she plucked faded heads off nasturtiums, daisies and geraniums, the garden suffering from her week in Toronto.

Back in the Vancouver days, Patrick had insisted that she had a special gift for seeing into people, for seeing them as they saw themselves. He had often encouraged her to give up her bookstore and put what he called her "impossible intuition" and her "uncanny perceptiveness" to work as a consultant. This could be done from his oceanside property on Galiano Island, where between bouts of work they could dwell together in rustic seclusion.

Patrick had been self-employed as a pilot, had kept his twin-engine amphibian tied to the small dock he had built in the protected lee of a nearby headland at Salamanca Point. In the winter months he flew helicopter on-call for the Coast Guard.

Nell had cherished the visits to Galiano and finally decided to give it a try. She took courses in conflict resolution and read everything she could get her hands on before selling the bookstore and leaving Vancouver. Suppressing an inborn reluctance to present herself as any kind of an expert, she had run a short ad in

2

the Vancouver and Victoria classifieds: "Conflict resolution services for workplace problems", with her phone number. To her surprise there had been several calls -- the first because two sanctimonious volunteers in a Nanaimo street shelter couldn't stand the sight of each other. Gradually she built on success through a diversity of problems -- from a travel agency, a supermarket, a local newspaper, a florist shop, a mining exploration business, through to larger companies and on to municipal and provincial government departments. She had once been called to an Ontario prison, there to defuse a powder-keg of tension that threatened a riot.

Finished now with the flowers, she picked basil and returned to the kitchen. She pulled tomatoes, free-range eggs, mushrooms, cheese, and garlic out of the fridge to build the mega-omelette that would keep her going until dinner.

Nell had learned a lot about people during her five years as a consultant. The most common problem, apart from the usual tunnel-vision that would yield to standard techniques, was cynicism. Cynicism and other negative emotions created twists in character that sent disturbing ripples through the workplace. These twists would colour the agendas of key people, and Nell found she had a kind of sixth sense in locating the source of the trouble. A demand grew up for her services. She began to refer the regular dispute work to other agencies, dealing with the more intriguing problems herself. In short, she was becoming something of a sleuth.

She poured coffee, served the omelette onto a hot ironstone plate and took her breakfast out to the balcony. Then, returning through the kitchen, she crossed to the living-room, opened the large windows that looked out over the balcony to the sea, and placed the Vivaldi mandolin concertos into the compact disc drive. Bright, lively, and crisply intricate, the music floated out through the windows onto the still morning air.

Plate in hand she reclined in a deck chair, eating slowly, savouring the food, and gazing across at the hard line of mountains on the Vancouver shore. To the east Mount Baker rose in whiteclad majesty above its shouldering hills. A peripheral movement caught her eye and she turned to see a large, very heavily furred, iron-grey cat with green eyes waft into sight from

3

around the corner of the house.

"Pelt!"

Pelt was obviously very put out by Nell's absence, for he walked straight past her into the house, a picture of scornful indifference and feline superiority. A few moments later, succumbing to his true feelings, he drifted back out and jumped onto her lap, purring loudly. Pelt had gained weight during the week. He was a rover and a favourite with several neighbours, each of whom fed him prodigiously whenever Nell was away.

The soft "chirrup" of the telephone sounded inside and Pelt trotted after her as she entered the kitchen.

"Nell, it's Sonia. I've been cooped up all week, spinning wool. I'm dying for a game of tennis."

Nell had been looking forward to a solitary day sorting through the mail and doing a little gunkholing in the kayak, but the week in Toronto had afforded little chance for exercise, so she acquiesced.

"I could use a set or two. Pick you up in half an hour? I'll collect Rainforest when I come."

"Sure thing," said Sonia. "See you then."

Sonia was Nell's best friend on Galiano, and was married to Paul Willis, a surveyor who had left his job in Victoria and purchased a hundred-acre tract of forest land on Galiano to become a horse-logger. Paul and Sonia had two children, Jenny, six, and Michael, three. Sonia, on top of being a mother, raised chickens, goats, and sheep, and knitted heavy grey and brown sweaters from the wool.

Sonia and Nell had taken an instant liking to one another when the Willis' had moved to Galiano two years ago. They admired each other's different lives, complemented one another, and shared a common love of tennis.

Today, as usual, they wore their tennis whites. They got kidded for this eccentricity, for such it was in the rural ambience of this rugged and sparsely populated island. But they were strong, evenly matched players, and the whites somehow honed their determination. Nell had known moments of a suspended egoless state in which she could do no wrong. An unknown inner player would awaken and perfection seemed simply to happen, stroke after stroke of effortless harmony with the game. Sonia would fall into it too, and after such matches they would emerge on a triumphant and excited high, whichever had won. "*It* happened," Sonia would grin. "As the Zen masters would say, 'Let *it* happen!'"

Sonia was looking tanned and rested when she climbed into Nell's dusty green jeep, christened "the buggy" by Jenny. Paul and the kids had gone off to a swap-meet in search of tools. The women drove to the courts and got on immediately. Nell, jetlagged from her trip and the stormy night, couldn't find her game, and Sonia trounced her soundly, 6-3, then 6-2.

"I've got your number now," grinned Sonia. "I'll play you the mornings after business trips. Come back for a cup of tea?"

"Love a cup. It's the only way you'll ever win!"

As they bounced into the driveway and pulled up behind Paul's pick-up, the two children tore excitedly out of the barn, where their father had been grooming the team. Paul emerged smiling and nodded in the direction of a heavy-duty rototiller in pristine condition.

"Two hundred dollars," he beamed. "It's worth twice that."

This meant a much larger garden for the Willis's next spring, and a lot less back-breaking work. Sonia jumped forward with a cry of delight and deluged her husband with hugs and kisses. Paul, a rather serious and reserved Rhode Islander, glanced at Nell in mild embarrassment over this outburst of spontaneity. Nell laughed. Paul was certainly a descendant of his New England forefathers. There he stood, tall, hardened by physical work, black-moustached, and momentarily uncomfortable. Very human, Sonia's man.

"Tea!" declared Sonia, and they single-filed into the great open room of the log house that Paul and Sonia had built with trees from their own land. Immediately Nell entered the room a high-pitched *"HEL-LOW!!"* burst from the far corner by the window. It was Rainforest, her beloved African grey parrot, a cheerful, loyal, intelligent friend. He clung to the door of the cage, clamouring to be picked up and reunited with his mistress. "I *love* you! I *love* you!"

"I have to remind myself that he's only a parrot," said Nell, placing him on her shoulder, "because he always speaks to the occasion."

"He really does," agreed Jenny. "I've noticed it all week."

"When parrots talk, they're only parroting," announced Sonia.

"That's right," agreed Paul. "When I say 'good morning', Jenny, it's because I'm human, I *know* it's morning. But when Rainforest says 'good morning' he only says it because I do -- he just copy-cats."

"Now cats are witless too," said Nell. "I thought *we* just say it because other people do!" Jenny nodded enthusiastically.

They sat down at the big pine table for tea and scones.

"How was Toronto?" asked Paul.

"The pace was incredible. People literally run from place to place. They rev their brains at computers all day, then dart away in their cars at night."

"What about the problem at the trust company?" asked Sonia.

"Embezzlement...head office was suspicious and hired me to play the role of a new vice-president, going around to meet the staff to promote corporate communication. I talked to nearly everyone. As it turned out, a trust officer and a senior accountant had been working a scam against single senior citizens in care facilities. They were moving funds from the seniors' accounts into a dummy mutual funds account, and creaming that off to a numbered account in Switzerland."

"Snakes!" hissed Sonia.

"Worse!" continued Nell. "They had both booked holidays to give them some lead time and were scheduled to transfer the rest of the mutual funds to Switzerland and skip out permanently in another week. A week ago a bright young junior accountant twigged to the dummy fund and began asking the senior accountant some awkward questions. Rather stupidly they tried to buy her off. She played along, waiting for her chance to blow the whistle, but not knowing how many people were involved or whom to trust."

"She could have called the police," suggested Paul.

"Or Revenue Canada...she didn't feel it was her place," said Nell, "and these two were keeping a close eye on her. I was pretty sure she knew something so I explained that a head office executive, Mr. George de Faye, had received a complaint from a relative of one of the investors and had hired me to look around. She then told me of her predicament and we decided that I would go on interviewing the whole staff as though she'd kept mum about it. The embezzlers were in a tight spot -- they obviously couldn't flee the country while I was going through my vice-president routine -- meeting everyone, encouraging views and suggestions, asking about computer security. Two plainclothes RCMP arrived on Wednesday afternoon at exactly two-thirty, carrying briefcases."

"One for each crook," mused Paul.

"Yes, and was it exciting! The senior accountant was out in the front office when they came in -- he slipped into the hallway and took to the stairs. By prearrangement I was out in the front office, sending a fax. I signalled to the police, and the young one gave chase, caught up with him before he reached the street, and handcuffed him inside the police car. The trust officer was arrested in his office and went quietly. They've both signed confessions and are in jail waiting for trial."

"Did they get the money back?" asked Sonia.

"They can't get at it in Switzerland but they can recommend a reduced sentence if the money's returned."

"Or throw away the keys if it isn't," said Paul.

"...to the bottom of Lake Ontario," agreed Nell. "The company's going to install software that will keep track of who makes the accounting entries. That'll put people like me out of business!"

Just then Michael came in to ask for a cookie. As he stood munching, eyes level with the table, his gaze came to rest on some violet pansies that Sonia had arranged in a clay pot, with bright green moss around them.

Michael brightened and pointed. "Fwow-ers!" he exclaimed excitedly, smiling up at Nell.

"Flow-ers, Michael!" said Sonia in a clear, deliberate tone.

"Fwow-ers," persisted the little boy, hopefully raising his eyebrows.

"FLOW-ers," repeated his mother, more loudly and clearly than before.

The eyes in the little face squinted with concentration and a terrible frown gripped his forehead. *"FWOW-ERS!"* he yelled.

Sonia sighed and shook her head.

Suddenly Michael's frown dissolved into a look of triumphant

7

delight.

"Never mind," he declared happily. "I just say *PWANT!*"

The three adults collapsed with laughter and the little boy, tickled with this latest evidence of his wonderful genius and charm, ran from the room to play with the dog.

On that note Nell rose to depart, Paul and Sonia seeing her to the door. Chickens scattered in all directions as the screen door slammed.

"Have you got any eggs to spare?" asked Nell, and Sonia produced a bulging carton. Nell paid her the customary three dollars and tooted goodbye as she backed out of the driveway, the parrot clinging to its perch in the cage beside her.

CHAPTER 2

Nell was home from the tennis match, curled up on the sofa going through mail, when the telephone rang.

A male voice, slow and deliberate: "I'm looking for Mrs. Nell O'Donovan."

"Speaking."

"My name is Edward Siegel and I'm sorry to be calling at such short notice, but there's an urgent situation I must discuss with you. Do you have a moment?"

"Well...yes," replied Nell, mildly alarmed at the gravity in the man's tone.

"I was referred to you by Morris Stockton, a good friend of mine who heard a first-hand account of how you handled that prison affair at Northwood last fall."

"Oh yes. Who told the story to Mr. Stockton?"

"The assistant prison superintendent, Mr. Wiles."

"Oh yes," said Nell, recalling the courage and judgement Wiles had used, outranked as he had been by the senior administrator.

"I am the director of a Canadian Government agency which is coordinating an international scientific project in Northern Ontario. I cannot give you the details over the telephone, nor have I been able to contact you this week from my office. We are having some difficulties of a confidential nature and I need someone I can trust, onsite, to keep an ear tuned to what is going on. Would this interest you, and if so, would you be able to come

9

immediately?"

Nell was taken aback. "Immediately? I just got in from Toronto last night. I was going to spend a week catching up on things here..."

"This can't wait a week," interjected Siegel. "We're on a tight schedule with this project and the problem we're having has been causing delays."

"Really," protested Nell. "I can't just drop everything to take on a totally unknown assignment, across the country, at the drop of a hat, on the strength of a telephone call..."

"Would it help if I were to fly to Vancouver tomorrow to brief you in person?" asked Siegel quickly, a tone of urgency in the careful voice.

"Well, if it's that important..." hesitated Nell, wishing to God that Mr. Wiles had not spoken to Mr. Stockton, nor Mr. Stockton to Mr. Siegel. A week of oceanfront tranquillity, puttering in the garden, was hanging by a thread.

"Can you be in Vancouver by lunchtime?" asked Siegel quickly.

Nell considered the early ferry she would have to catch and the hassle of driving to the city and parking. "Damn!" she thought.

"I can meet you in the airport in time for lunch," conceded Nell slowly, inwardly cursing her failed resolve.

"Excellent!" announced Siegel. "And *thank* you, Mrs. O'Donovan. I'll phone you as soon as I can to let you know my arrival time. I'll be dressed in a dark grey wool overcoat, carrying a black briefcase with a green umbrella between the handles. I'll have the Globe & Mail in the other hand. I wear a cap. I'm middle-aged, a shade portly, about six feet tall. Okay?"

"Yes, that should do it," replied Nell, wondering how many other businessmen might fit the description. "I'm five-foot-six, red hair..."

"Never mind," cut in Siegel, "I've seen your picture. I'll call you back," and he hung up.

Nell arose before dawn, splashed water on her face, slipped into the faded old jogging suit, and ran the four kilometres to Whaler Bay as the sky lightened. The still water, gunmetal on the way down, was yellowing as she returned. She showered, dressed for business, turned on the CD for Rainforest -- five hours of uninterrupted classical music, including the arias from La Boheme which always provoked a spirited accompaniment from the little bird – then grabbed a muffin, locked up, and reluctantly departed the fine Salamanca morning.

She arrived at the ferry parking lot in Sturdies Bay, surprisingly full this morning at 8:15. As she waited, thoughtfully munching on the blueberry muffin, excuses drifted into her mind for not being able to take on this assignment. Her bent was towards theatre, music, museums, and the outdoors; she had neither interest nor aptitude for science. She was not the right person for the job. She would explain this to Mr. Siegel, apologize in embarrassment for his wasted day, do some shopping in Richmond, and return home for her week of peace and quiet.

A ship's horn echoed around the bay just as the ferry slid into view from Active Pass, enroute from its previous stop at Village Bay on Mayne Island. It eased neatly between the pilings, the large metal ramp was lowered to the dock, and traffic of all kinds -- pick-ups, an ambulance, a telephone company vehicle, a moving truck, some surveyors in a light panel truck -- all lurched off the ramp and trundled up the long dock to their various destinations on Galiano. When the last car was off, the attendant waved the waiting traffic down the dock and balanced it in lanes on the ferry deck. Nell climbed the steps of the old Queen of Vancouver, an original member of the fleet, and took a front seat in the passenger lounge, where she spent the hour alternately working on correspondence and scanning the open waters of Georgia Strait.

About midway, the ferry slowed to allow a log-boom, attached by a long submerged cable to a tugboat, to pass in front. Nell flashed back to the summer, when two couples had chartered a sailboat, and on a perfectly clear and windless day had powered between two distant vessels, a tug running with the current on their port side, and a barge on their starboard. The cable had caught between the keel and the rudder, the sailboat had been swept along it and run down by the looming, implacable barge. The women had been making lunch below; the men were in the cockpit drinking beer. All four had jumped overboard, one drowning before help arrived. Nell remembered that Patrick, a man who liked his drink, would never touch it while flying or sailing.

The ferry arrived at the Tsawwassen terminal on time, and Nell occupied the two hours before her meeting with Siegel at the Richmond Public Library, catching up on world news, running to ground a recipe for Thai chicken, and choosing some light novels for her coming week of well-earned leisure.

Then she headed for the airport, realizing en route that in spite of the long morning run and the preoccupations of the library, she had a case of the jitters. Usually a run would settle her mind and body into a whole day of quiet stability. Dr. Morrow, her GP, had explained that running burnt off the adrenalin that the stresses of ordinary life built up in the bloodstream, but it certainly wasn't working today. Nell had a premonition that this assignment was going to be difficult -- difficult to refuse and difficult to complete. She worked on more excuses. She was tired, she needed a holiday: if she had to give up this precious week she would charge twice her usual rate and full expenses to boot.

The airport parking was a nightmare. Cars everywhere: circling, swooping, braking, honking. She spotted one at the far end, and managed to arrive, a little flustered, in the arrivals lounge just as the first passengers appeared from the Air Canada flight that Mr. Siegel had caught on standby.

Nell composed herself by firmly resolving to end the interview as expeditiously as possible, and then stood calmly waiting. A few moments later, an unmistakable Mr. Siegel emerged, limping slightly, and carrying the stated items. His step quickened when he saw her, and he crossed the lounge with dignified alacrity, arm outstretched to shake hands.

"Mrs. O'Donovan, how do you do? Thank you very much for coming."

His handshake was reassuring. "Welcome to our West Coast autumn," she laughed. There had been reports of snow in Toronto that morning. "Did they give you lunch on the plane?"

"Just breakfast and a snack so I'm ready for lunch," he replied. "Last time I was in Vancouver Airport I found some delicious Mexican food. I wonder if it's still around?"

"Yes, it's upstairs," said Nell, resigned to having at least a quick bite before leaving. "How was your flight?"

"Slow. The milk run. Two stops. I've been up since 4:00 this morning."

They found the bistro and were soon seated, he with a bottle of beer and Nell with tea, waiting for the enchiladas.

"Well, Mrs. O'Donovan, let me put you into the picture. The project I represent is called the Canadian Neutrino Project, alias CNP. Have you heard of it?"

"No," replied Nell. "Never. What's an utreeno?"

Siegel smiled and shook his head. "N-e-u-t-r-i-n-o," he spelled. "It's a tiny subatomic particle, orders of magnitude smaller than an electron, but it has no charge. It's neutral -- hence neutrino. It was named by an Italian physicist called Fermi back in 1933. It's Italian for 'little neutral one'."

"Yes, I remember that electrons were negative and protons were positive. But I got terrible marks in science -- I really didn't want to know." She flicked a smile at the gracious young Chinese waiter bearing salads.

Siegel looked at the level, determined eyes of the young woman across the table and knew that she did not want any part of this assignment. She had done everything but look at her watch.

"Please listen carefully, Mrs. O'Donovan. I have a real problem. There are four governments involved in this project -- Canada, the US, Britain, and Italy. And there are dozens of physicists on board. Seventy-five million dollars have been poured into the project with more to come. But the problem is not the neutrinos, it's the people who are studying them."

"Oh," said Nell flatly, not wishing to feel or betray any curiosity whatsoever.

"Before I go on I must have your guarantee of absolute silence in this matter," said Siegel, looking hard at Nell. "It cannot be discussed with anyone. If you decide not to take the assignment, you must forget everything I tell you -- just wipe it out of your mind."

Nell frowned and put down her fork. "Is this project dangerous? If it is, Mr. Siegel, I'm not sure I *want* to know anything."

"So far no one has been hurt, but there are no guarantees."

"Matters involving risk should be referred to the police."

"I don't want to bring in the police just yet, and I sincerely hope that it won't come to that. This is a delicate situation, involving people with great distinction in the international scientific community. If I can solve the problem in-house without the media getting wind of it, I can avoid public embarrassment for the project."

"I see," said Nell slowly. "What exactly do you want me to do?"

"I need someone who can fit into the project in a legitimate working role, someone who will not cause suspicion or alarm, but whose real function will be to observe what is going on between the physicists."

"But I wouldn't understand the first word of it!" she protested.

"That's not the point," replied Siegel with a quiet smile. "What you are to look out for is something unusual or obsessive -- passion, intensity, rigidity, fear perhaps -- someone who cares too much about the outcome of the project. Someone who..."

"...might wish to sabotage it?" she put in.

Siegel looked at the grey-green eyes and replied lightly, "Something like that, yes."

The enchiladas arrived, steaming hot, smothered in cheese and tomato sauce. Siegel smiled broadly for the first time. "I take it you would be willing to hear my story, Mrs. O'Donovan?"

"I will listen, but no promises."

"Good!" exclaimed Siegel heartily. "We'll find somewhere to talk later. Now let us enjoy this fine lunch!" and he beckoned to the waiter for another glass of beer.

Siegel and Nell worked their way through the lunchtime bistro crowd to the cashier, then out into the pale afternoon sunshine.

"How long will you be in Vancouver?" queried Nell.

"I'm staying over at the Delta Inn and taking an early flight back tomorrow," replied Siegel. "Where can we talk?"

"It's a lovely afternoon -- we could take a walk around the Reifel Bird Sanctuary on Westham Island. It's not far from here."

"Fine. This game leg doesn't bother me much. We'll need an hour or two."

They drove in silence to the island, paid the admission and entered the main trail. At first they walked quietly, taking in the autumn fragrance of the fallen leaves beneath their feet, which blended sweetly with the sea air drifting in from the the coast. Nell would have loved to peer about in search of birds as she had so often done with Patrick, but Siegel, assured now of privacy and no interruptions, came to the point.

"Mrs. O'Donovan, the neutrino is the tiniest yet most numerous particle in the universe. We're not even sure it's a particle -- it may be more like a wave. Most people have never even heard of it, but at the moment it's at the heart of a deep and divisive controversy in astrophysics and particle physics. And we believe that very soon, when the CNP gets underway, we shall solve the mystery once and for all."

"How can it be so important if no one's ever heard of it?"

Siegel looked askance. "Well, that's not exactly true, Mrs. O'Donovan. Probably ten percent of people, if asked, would tell you that it was a quark or something. But for years now, while most of us have been going about our daily business, something incredible that seldom gets into the news has been going on behind the scenes..."

"You said that I wouldn't have to understand neutrinos, only people," she broke in, risking further irritation.

"Yes, but to understand the feelings and motivations of these physicists you will have to know what's at stake for them," he replied. "The story is actually very simple. Intriguing, too. And the positions people take on the controversy reveal a great deal about their mindsets in general."

"Is something big about to change?" asked Nell.

"It's probable that what we learn in the next year will revolutionize our understanding of the whole physical universe."

"And this will upset people."

"It's bound to. Those who have made their names by the old theories will be overshadowed," he replied. "Of course particle physics is mostly theory anyway. These theories are large mathematical models that can be moulded around known events like putty. People get committed to these models -- they are their creations, their livelihoods, and their reputations as well."

"I may have difficulty following you..."

"Not a chance! The story would delight a child of ten," beamed Siegel. "I guarantee you'll find this as fascinating a tale as

15

you've ever heard."

His enthusiasm was infectious. "Proceed!" laughed Nell, with the first real interest she had felt all day.

"We shall sit on this bench near the pigeons then, and please interrupt me if you feel a chill."

CHAPTER 3

"The neutrino is sometimes called the 'ghost particle' of physics. As I was uttering the words 'ghost particle', billions of neutrinos were shooting right through us, through the bench we're sitting on, and through the rocks below -- all at the speed of light. They zoom through solid objects like bullets through butter.

"Neutrinos are more numerous than photons, the particles that carry light," he continued. "But they seldom hit anything because they're next to nothing themselves. And because they're neutral in charge there is no attracting them so they just keep on going.

"Even neutrinos will sometimes interact with other particles, but when they do, it is very weakly. They are the *only* particle which interacts *only* via the weak force, which makes them a unique tool in the study of elemental forces -- but I digress...."

"Where do they come from?" asked Nell, promoting simplicity.

"Mostly from the sun and other stars -- they are the only entity capable of escaping the dense core of the sun. Let me tell you how we have been trying to capture them.

"Imagine a huge, ten-storey tank located two kilometres deep in the earth -- that's nearly a mile and a half straight down -- about 7500 feet. A ten-storey building is about 100 feet high. We're talking about major construction at a depth equivalent to 75 ten-storey buildings."

"How in heaven do you get down that far? It's hard enough to drill a well down 200 feet!"

17

"We're using a mineshaft from an old abandoned nickel mine outside Sudbury, Ontario. We hired ten miners to blast out an enormous barrel-shaped underground cavern, itself 12 storeys high and 10 storeys wide. Some of that rock was dumped in the mine, but most of it had to be brought to the surface."

"It must have taken forever!"

"The excavation phase took nearly three years," replied Siegel. "Now we're nearing completion of phase two, the observatory itself, which has taken another two years. The heart of the observatory is an acrylic tank which will hold 200,000 gallons of heavy water -- that's a thousand tonnes. This is being supplied at cost by the Canadian government and will be trucked in and pumped down the shaft and then along about two hundred metres of tunnel to the tank."

"I saw a World War II movie about smuggling heavy water, but I don't remember why it was so valuable..."

"Heavy water -- or deuterium -- has a double neutron in the hydrogen atom, so it's more likely that a neutrino will collide with it than with ordinary water."

"How can a neutrino collide with anything?"

"We know from past experiments in other countries that a very small percentage of neutrinos will chance to strike other particles. The neutrino was long thought to be *almost* a nothing, a speck of a particle, or a minute wave of energy, perhaps -- but now we're not so sure. And it's important to know what they actually are, because the universe is literally teeming with them. They are so abundant that collectively they could account for the missing dark matter of the universe, and if so, they will be the clue to the fate of the universe."

Nell turned to face Siegel. "How can you tell when they collide?"

"When they strike a particle in heavy water, the energy from the impact is released as a tiny flash of blue light -- Cerenkov light. From the number of flashes that register on the equipment we can project the approximate total coming through."

Nell grinned. "I see myself sitting on the edge of the Indian Ocean on a balmy moonlit night, staring intently into the water, counting pinpoints of phosphorescence."

"Or counting fireflies in the dark," added Siegel. "Actually, what we do is very technical. We catch these little sparks in reflectors, then we photograph them. The whole outside of the tank will be lined with banks of these detectors, about ten thousand of them. But there's a problem. Background radiation -- from the surrounding rock, the cement casing, and even from the reflectors and photomultiplier tubes themselves. All this material emits radiation which produces light."

"So what's the point, then?"

"There will be some very sophisticated computers in the control room, programmed to separate the neutrino sparks from the rest of the cosmic clutter. By 'clutter' I mean two to five billion interactions a day, versus a few dozen neutrino hits."

Nell sat gazing a Siegel, shaking her head in wonderment, saying nothing.

"But we're minimizing the background radiation as much as possible -- using special aluminum in the reflectors, special steel for the superstructure, special glass in the photomultipliers, special concrete -- special everything.

"Then there's the further problem of other cosmic rays from space which can also penetrate the two kilometres of rock to steal the show from the neutrinos. And there's the thorium radiation from the rock itself. To silence all this static, we're surrounding the acrylic tank with an outside sphere of ultrapure water -- nearly eight thousand tonnes of it. The core of our observatory will be the lowest-radioactivity site in the world."

Nell sat back, frowning slightly. "How is all this so important to the fate of the earth?"

At that moment the sky darkened as a magnificent flock of snow geese, black-tipped wings beating in slow precision, wheeled in from the sea to glide to the fields beyond.

Siegel held his breath in awe as he witnessed this stunning phenomenon for the first time. Shielding his eyes from the sun, he was drawn to his feet in astonishment, and then along the path to better view the masses of white birds, which continued to arrive in staggering numbers.

"They're snow geese!" shouted Nell, following.

He turned after a moment, eyes excited. "I've never seen the like of it!"

"They spend the summer on Wrangel Island in Siberia and in

19

late October they migrate to the Fraser Delta here to winter."

"So *many!*"

"About 25,000 in total -- they've probably been here a few days. At low tide they feed down at the shore, and when the tide comes in they move up to the fields to forage."

"I've lost my train of thought," he said, reseating himself.

"I was just asking how neutrinos can be so important to the fate of the earth," she said. "Will they effect these snow geese? I thought the fate of the world was in human hands these days."

"We astrophysicists think long-term," replied Siegel, "and we strongly suspect that neutrinos will provide the clue to the future -- whether the universe will continue expanding indefinitely, or whether the enormous collective weight of its neutrinos will cause it to snap back gravitationally upon itself, like a big elastic band. We look to that distant day, billions of years off, when the sun will burn out and when the Big Bang that created the universe may reverse itself into the Big Crunch. But by that time both humans and snow geese will have evolved into new life forms, if, as you suggest, we humans don't wreck it all in the meantime. Now, have I piqued your curiosity enough to continue with the story?"

"Yes. I'm intrigued. Shall we walk down to the observation tower?"

Nell and Siegel found the tower unoccupied, climbed its metal frame, and stood high-up looking out over the marshlands to the ocean, now cold blue in the November light. The sea air was crisp on their faces and the wintry limbs of maple and alder reached skeletally through brilliant rags of leaves.

"Over 50 years ago a man called Hans Bethe earned himself a future Nobel Prize by explaining the hydrogen fusion that powers the stars of our galaxy, including the sun. His model has become the cornerstone of modern astrophysics -- it explains how hotly stars burn, how long they live, how their nuclear furnaces create oxygen, carbon, iron, and all the elements that make up the surrounding planets and indeed life itself. His theory has become known as the 'Standard Solar Model'."

"A widely accepted model but still a theory?" suggested Nell.

"That's right. It's a beautiful, consistent theory and no one wants it to fail. But there's a serious problem. We can only count

20

one-third the number of neutrinos that the standard solar model predicts should be reaching earth from the centre of the sun. Something is wrong with our physics -- either with the neutrino or with our understanding of the sun itself -- and it's a thorn in the side of astrophysicists. It dominates every conference. A cloud has passed between us and our knowledge of the sun, casting a shadow over a great deal of established work. This new observatory is designed to give us an accurate count and thereby clear up the controversy."

"A poor result would mean a lot of rebuilding, then -- the theoretical equivalent of a flood or earthquake," she mused.

"Right again -- if the low neutrino counts are confirmed. So it comes as no real surprise that attempts have been made to sabotage our observatory."

"How do I fit in?" asked Nell.

"We'll get to that, but first let me run through the 'accidents' that have occurred. First, a large supply of dynamite was soaked during a rainfall. Someone had removed some shingles from the warehouse. We chalked that up to local environmental resistance to a major project.

"Next came a breakdown in the elevator control panel -- somebody pried it open and brutalized it, just before the night watchman came on duty at six p.m. The panel was a specialty item for the project and its replacement had to be built from scratch. This cost us a week or two, and we began to suspect there was determined resistance to the project.

"We brought the night watchman on at four o'clock. Then one lunch-hour six crates of photomultiplier tubes were pushed off the top of the stockpile in the reassembly lab and smashed. These again were specialty items and we had to go back to the Italian manufacturer for replacements. We lost a month. Then, to top things off, the big network server was destroyed with a large magnet before it was even unpacked. It had just been delivered to the warehouse and was awaiting inspection by Alex Wong. We had to replace the drives, the operating system, the software, everything. That cost a week."

"How's your security? Could activists get into these areas?"

"The compound is fenced, guarded, and locked at night," replied Siegel. "It's got to be someone on the project. So I need

21

someone else on the project, someone who fits in and won't cause suspicion, to be my eyes and ears. There are two jobs vacant right now that you could plausibly fill. One's a waitress in the cafeteria, the other's the administrative assistant to the chief project engineer. I'd have to pull some strings."

"I have a PC with Windows at home," replied Nell, "and I worked one summer as a waitress during high school."

"Hmmm...the office admin job could get you down to the computer control room in the mine. It would also put you in touch with the physicists."

Recalling the terror she'd faced in the underground caves at Horne Lake, Vancouver Island, she felt a flutter of apprehension at the thought of riding down that mineshaft. Siegel saw the freeze in her eyes and quickly corrected. "A lot of people won't go down. It's like flying, or long highway bridges -- the primeval fear of being trapped. I'll try to make sure you don't go down unless you're easy with it."

Nell relaxed, smiling faintly, grateful for the kindness of this neutrino project director. "I'll go down if I have to," she declared, hoping the promise would give her the nerve.

CHAPTER 4

"Will that be tea or coffee, Ma'am?"

Nell awoke from her reverie to see the green and white clad flight attendant smiling over her, steaming pots in both hands.

She glanced at her watch: eight p.m. Galiano time, eleven o'clock in Toronto. They'd be landing in an hour. "Tea, please, or I won't sleep a wink."

The little white-haired lady on her left, in the window seat, opted for tea as well. The two women had enjoyed a companionable dinner together, and now the elder remarked, "Only an hour to go. For years I spent the last hour in jitters over landing. I used to do a lot of flying and finally gave in to tranquilizers. That was before I discovered the *secret.*"

Nell perked up. "What secret?"

"I met a man up here -- a passenger, that is -- who noticed my white knuckles. He was a biochemist en route to a conference, to deliver a paper on oils in human nutrition. What he told me has changed my life." The old lady smiled broadly, her blue eyes sparkling with satisfaction.

"Oils in human nutrition?" queried Nell politely. The old lady had been surprisingly knowledgeable on a good many subjects. Maybe she had something.

"Yes. Essential fatty acids, to be sure. Our brains and nervous systems are made of them. But the trouble is, we don't get enough of the right kind of them in our diet any more. This young man believed that this deficiency accounts for the current epidemic in nervous system diseases -- MS, ALS, Alzheimer's, Parkinson's, depression, chronic fatigue, panic attacks -- you name it."

Nell was tired, but this was just intriguing enough. "What do you mean, 'the right kind of them'?"

"In the good old days, when we lived close to the land, the cattle we ate grazed on grass, and our fish fed on smaller fish which ate algae. Grass and algae use green chlorophyll cells to build themselves into solid carbohydrate plants, using no more than sunlight, carbon dioxide, and water. Today our beef cattle are fed corn and grain, not the elemental green grasses they used to eat. Those happily grazing animals of yore produced two kinds of fatty acids which are essential to our health -- omega-3's and omega-6's. The ratio between them was about 50-50."

"I was never any good at science," confessed Nell, sighing inwardly and thinking of Siegel.

"This is simplicity itself!" urged her companion, a little conspiratorially. "These days, with grain-fed beef and farmed fish, we get 96% omega-6's, but only 4% omega-3's. Now here's the kicker. The brain and nervous system are *made* of omega-3's! *Made* of them! Not only that! The large, low-density cholesterols that cause plaques and hardening of the arteries and heart attacks come from too much omega-6!"

"The brain is made of omega-3 oils?" repeated Nell incredulously.

"Absolutely. And when I began to supplement my diet with them -- with fish oils and canola oil and flaxseed oil and evening primrose oil -- I stopped being nervous on airplanes!"

"It's worth a try," said Nell, reaching for her pen and notebook. There was something very real and kind about this woman. Nell dug further into her purse and produced her business card.

"The time has passed quickly talking to you," she said warmly. "I would be very pleased if you would contact me if you ever come to the Gulf Islands."

"Indeed I shall! My name is Betty Sable. I live in a flat in the outskirts of Toronto. I'm the only one in the book. You must come and stay with me!"

With a sudden change in their momentum, Nell felt the

familiar barb of adrenalin in her solar plexus; they had begun their descent. She looked over to the old lady, who smiled reassuringly, then laughed.

"I'll definitely try those omega-3's," Nell promised herself. In a short time they touched down smoothly and the two women walked together to the baggage claims, shook hands, and parted.

Nell awoke Sunday morning on the twelfth floor of the Friendly Skies Inn and rang down for the continental breakfast, which arrived just as she emerged from the shower, dressed for winter. It was November 7th. As she struggled with the little plastic knife to deal with the cardboard Danish she tuned to the road report, which was forecasting flurries on 400 and north. She sipped stale acidic coffee to wash down the cardboard. Then she fitted her key-ring with the car and apartment keys she had picked up at the reception desk last night. Her motoring identity was a used Tercel, 4-WD. Sensible. Good for the winter roads.

She re-read Siegel's couriered note giving the location of her apartment in Sudbury, and the name of the project manager she was to contact on Monday morning. A month's rent had been paid on a small unassuming duplex in an outlying residential neighbourhood. The official story was that she had lost her husband in a freak skiing accident outside Vancouver and had come east to start a new life. Any lapses or confusions on her part could be put down to the widow in mourning. She had retained her own name during the marriage, which made her Nell Fitzgerald again.

In the envelope was a copy of the job description she had applied for and a letter appointing her to the six-month maternity leave position. Siegel had been pulling strings in Ottawa; her new life was coming together. Why she was interested in neutrinos or in living in Sudbury had been left to her.

Nell rode the elevator to the basement parkade and loaded her "life possessions" into the back of the station wagon. Two big suitcases and a flight bag. Better start getting into the role, she thought; the widow part would be easy.

The Tercel started immediately and Nell snaked her way out of the labyrinthine basement. She had sold her Beetle convertible to block out past associations -- it was not a car for winter anyway. Then she had flown to Toronto to buy something more suitable. Fine. These offhand lies came to her with alarming readiness.

In her own life she had cleaved to everything she and Patrick had shared, but it takes all kinds to make a world; others would see her as tortured and heart-broken for running away. Good -- she would allow herself to go quiet and stare pensively into space.

Out on the highway traffic was light, freezing rain was turning to snow, the wipers slapping time to Bobby McGee as the vehicle slushed through the wintry landscape. Nell felt the old longing rise up and wondered how long it would take to solve the neutrino puzzle. How long before she could return to Galiano, to home, where in some odd way she was still married to Patrick.

She forced her mind back to the present. Why in God's name do you want to work in a neutrino observatory, anyway? Because I heard all about it on Morningside. It will put Canada on the cutting edge of astrophysics and that will look good on a resume. And it looks like good cross-country skiing in these parts and that's why I came here in winter. It's all settled, then, I'm plausible -- and I've never even been to Galiano.

She drove into The Rock at twilight. The place had a surprisingly big-city feel, with lights coming on in the dusk and everything under a comfortable blanket of fresh snow. In the distance the low hills crouched in hazy anonymity beneath the dying light.

Nell pulled in for gas and groceries and asked the way to the apartment.

"Over behind the Memorial Hospital." He drew a little map. "When you get over to Regent, hang a left, then a right at McLeod, then another left. You can't miss it. You'll love it here!"

That ready open cheerfulness of the Canadian north. A century of building this old CPR town, pulling together against the harsh winters and the spring mud and the isolation and the blackflies. Nell had got her hands on a centennial review of the city, which claimed that Sudbury had outgrown its mining adolescence and emerged a mature, clean, modern city, economically strong, and boasting one of the ten best lifestyles in the country. The "Toronto of the North". We shall see, thought

Nell, pulling up to the brick duplex.

The double lock turned heavily and she entered a freshly painted furnished apartment with polished floors and area rugs. Fumbling for lights she carried the groceries and flight bag into the kitchen and set them down. She checked the phone; its dialtone echoed through the empty kitchen. She turned up the heat, smiled satisfaction at the spotless bathroom and clawfoot tub, found the firm bed. Quiet, secure, and comfortable, this would serve well as a base. Good for Siegel.

Nell, weary from her travels, tossed together sockeye, rice, lemon and greens, then nodded through the CBC news and betook herself to the firm bed. Without a thought for the morrow she plunged into the soundest of sleeps.

♦

"Ms. Fitzgerald?" barked a male voice.

Nell had been reading the Sudbury Star in the reception area outside the office of the project engineer. She rose to shake the offered hand and followed him into his office.

"I'm Bridges, I'm in charge of this project. Have a seat."

Mike Bridges was a solid man in his early forties. Auzzie accent. Crisp white shirt, tie and collar open at the neck with a mat of dark hair showing; a lean determined face and no-nonsense manner. He came straight to the point.

"Getting you in here was Siegel's idea. I wanted the police but he preferred a lower profile."

"It wouldn't be Scotland Yard," Nell observed easily.

"RCMP special investigators. I thought they might scare the bastard off but Siegel wants to play it low-key with the scientists, now that it's looking like inside work."

"What's the official explanation?"

"We had the local police in over the warehouse roof and the elevator panel. They figured local vandals or environmental activists and suggested stepping up security. We're saying the smashed photomultipliers was an accident in transit. As for the big computer server, there was a pretty blue flash when we turned it on. It was dead and we sent it back."

"So now you've got me here and we're waiting for the next

27

accident?"

"That's about it. As my administrative assistant you'll have the run of the place, above and below ground. Siegel tells me you're easy with people and they open up to you."

"I try to see people as they see themselves," acknowledged Nell.

"What do you do when they're lyin' through their teeth?"

"That takes acting skill and a good memory. They usually slip up."

"You're in that position yourself," challenged Bridges.

"I suppose I am!" laughed Nell. "But I have the advantage. I'm new and above suspicion -- a maternity-leave replacement from across the country."

"I'll grant you that," replied Bridges, "but any more of these incidents and we *will* be high profile -- *way* behind our opening schedule. I doubt you'll get any confessions. Now I'd better show you around."

Bridges led Nell through a connecting door to the left of his desk into a smaller office. "You'll spend a lot of time in here," he remarked. "You'll be on the phone a lot, and you'll be e-mailing and faxing for specialty items from those books over there." He nodded towards a bookshelf stuffed with catalogues. "You'll be receiving shipments and signing goods-received and delivering components up and down the shaft."

"Mr. Bridges..." began Nell in protest.

"Mike's the name. You'll be making travel arrangements for the scientists coming and going, and getting them into the dorms over there..."

There was a knock at his door. "Come in! Oh hullo, Jack. This is Nell Fitzgerald from Vancouver, Sue's replacement. Jack Suhara -- my right-hand man -- the assistant project engineer."

A short, dapper Suhara bowed and smiled blandly at Nell.

"Sue has been gone one week and we are lost without her. Welcome!"

Bridges continued. "Jack is on loan to us from the Kuchino project in Japan. Jack, would you show Ms. Fitzgerald the ropes around here?"

"Please, call me Nell," she said to both of them.

"Right." Bridges looked at his watch. "I've got a meeting over at Laurentian with some of the team. Jack, give Nell some coffee, introduce her to Mrs. Higgins, get her working on this stack of paper, and then take her over to the cafeteria for lunch. I'll introduce her to the others this afternoon."

Jack nodded stiff assent to these rather terse instructions. Bridges grabbed briefcase, jacket, and parka, and strode from the office.

"Do you take cream and sugar?" asked Jack.

"Black, please," replied Nell, seating herself before the computer. Jack disappeared momentarily, then returned with coffee.

"Bring your coffee and meet Mrs. Higgins, our stenograher," said Jack, leading her across the hall into the general office. Seated at a computer was a grey-haired woman in a red sweater, squinting at a sheet of yellow foolscap bearing handwritten notes.

Jack's stilted introduction was interrupted by the woman. "I sure hope you have a clear hand, young woman." She waved the page meaningully at Nell. "Some of the folks around here write in hieroglypics, and I'm no Egyptian!"

"It seems you run a tight ship," said Nell with a twinkle.

"If you need to send a fax or make a photocopy just speak to Mrs. Higgins," put in Jack.

"Sue prepared a little manual on how to do her job," said Mrs Higgins, handing it to Nell. "It will tell you how to log onto the computer and open your e-mail. The system will prompt you for your ID, NellFitz, and your password, which has been temporarily set as 'dustmite'."

"Thank you, Mrs. Higgins -- the manual will make things much easier," she replied. They returned to Nell's office.

"Now I must go to the observatory," said Jack. He walked over to a filing cabinet and pointed to an inbasket piled high with assorted papers. "This is the work that has been piling up since Sue left. Do your best with it. See you later."

As Nell was perusing the manual, the telephone rang on Jack's line.

"Nell Fitzgerald speaking."

"Oh, you're the new admin officer replacing Sue," replied a cheerful female voice. "I'm Biz Castle, on the systems team. I'm down in the control room setting up some of the lab computers.

We're missing a sound-board in the new Pentium. Could you find the packing slip -- it would have arrived last Thursday or so -- and call the firm in Toronto? We'll need to have it flown in this afternoon if they can manage it."

"Sure, OK," said Nell. "I'll get back," and she took the control room number.

Nell hunted around and found the invoice and packing slip, on which all of the components, including a sound-board, had been ticked off and initialled by an A.W. Not another "accident", surely? She called Toronto. Yes, they had the missing board in stock and would put it on a late morning flight, no charge, they appreciated the business. She called down to a grateful Biz who said that Alex Wong, the head of Systems, could easily have pirated the sound-board for another computer, he was prone to that sort of thing. Whew! Too early to run headlong into another delay, no sooner had Bridges left the office.

Jack collected her early, in time to avoid the lunchroom rush. The Monday Special was sushi, an unexpected treat. They chose a table by the window and were soon joined by Biz Castle and Alex Wong. The two were engaged in a lively argument over parts procedures as they approached the table.

"You must be the lady who saved my day," smiled a petite, freckled Biz. "Jack, you're lucky to have this woman! Nell, meet my boss, Alex Wong."

"Hi! Very pleased to meet you!" beamed a relaxed and cordial systems manager out of his square Chinese face. A good personality to head up a complex computer system, thought Nell, with all its quirks and foibles. But as the sushi arrived he suddenly remembered an errand, excused himself, and left the table.

CHAPTER 5

Nell had sorted the backlog on her desk into a kind of triage, having dealt with the most urgent matters by the time Mike Bridges stormed back into the office late at 3:00.

"There's a goddamn strike looming with the truckers. They want to start bringing the ultrapure on bloody Thursday and we won't be ready for it until Saturday at the earliest. Christ almighty! The damn unions are *running* this country!"

"What can I do to help?" asked Nell equably. "Could I call some of the other trucking lines?"

"It's a huge job, it's going to take tankers around the clock for the better part of a week to haul that water in here and pump it down. You can't arrange a contract like that at the drop of a hat!"

"Lot's of businesses use tankers," thought Nell out loud. "Oil companies, propane distributors, milk producers..."

"By God you may have hit it!" yelled Bridges. "There's a big dairy farm down around Belleville that went belly-up last month. They may have trucks available, and need some cash to boot...what the hell was the name of it?" he frowned, scratching his jaw. "That's it! Lakeview Farms! Get the number for me, would you?"

"Yessir," as she dialled Information, returning a moment later with the number.

He motioned Nell to wait while he made the call.

"The trucks are being sold, you say? How many are there? Sixteen?...that would do us...you laid off the drivers? Any chance you could lease those trucks to us and contact your drivers? We need them on Saturday for four or five days to haul water from

31

the tanks in Toronto to the project here in Sudbury. OK, you find out and I'll see if I can get contract approval...I'll call you in an hour...yes, thanks." He hung up, excited now, all fury abated.

"Well it just might work. I've gotta talk to Siegel -- he'll probably have to call the Minister," and he grabbed the telephone again. Nell returned to her office.

For the next hour Nell could hear Bridges' emphatic voice explaining this, urging that, but at the end of it all he appeared in the doorway, satisfied. "Good idea, the milk tankers -- doubt I would have thought of it. Now the next thing is that the physicists will be arriving on Wednesday for another workshop. They'll be here a week this time. You'll be meeting them all over dinner and drinks."

"How often do they meet here?"

"Oh, a couple of days every month or so to discuss progress on the project. And neutrino readings at the other observatories, in the US, Japan, Italy. They review the new theoretical papers as well."

"What about the 'accidents'? Were the scientists here then?"

"Yes, in each case most of the regulars were here. Of course there's nothing conclusive about that -- anyone could have used their visits as a cover."

"I expect you have a record of who was here on those dates?"

"I've listed all the physicists and engineers, and the dates involving vandalism that each was here," he answered, unlocking a drawer in his desk. He passed her some handwritten notes on yellow foolscap.

"Make a copy in Mrs. Higgins' office and bring back the originals. Keep it to yourself -- better take it home with you. Now, I've got to get working on this contract with Lakeview. We'll try to get to your tour of the place tomorrow."

Following an early dinner, Nell curled up in the rocker and dug the foolscap notes out of her purse. Bridges' brisk scrawl covered several pages:

VANDALISM DATES

1) *Thursday August 8th. Elevator panel thrashed before night watchman came on duty at 18:00. Workshop going all day Thursday and Friday.*
2) *Friday September 6th. Photomultipliers smashed at noon in reassembly lab. Workshops going all day Thursday and Friday.*
3) *Thursday October 3rd. Computer drive wiped out with a magnet in the warehouse. Workshops Thursday and Friday.*

THOSE PRESENT ON ABOVE DATES

Dr. Carl Hoffman, Dept. of Astrophysics, UCLA. Widely published supporter of big crunch theory, that neutrinos have mass and account for dark matter. Believes in MSW. Dates: all 3.

"How am I going to remember all this?" mused Nell. "Oh well...Carl and crunch."

Dr. Robin Kettering, Dept. of Religious Studies, University of British Columbia. Specialist in Buddhism, the philosophy of enlightenment, and its parallels with quantum mechanics. Cosmologist -- the astrophysical study of the structure and dynamics of the universe. Dates: 1 and 2

Lots of robins around UBC...

Dr. Moira Houston, Astronomy Dept, Univ. Virginia. Well-known supernova specialist. Believes in MSW; forecasts high counts on the new equipment. Dates: All 3.

M...? Moira and MSW? Whatever that is...

Dr. Sidney Hawthorpe, Dept. of Physics, Pennsylvania State

33

U. Working on a grand unification theory, a single force that would explain all the laws of nature. Dates: all 3

Sidney and single force...more alliteration...

Dr. Cam MacAllister, Queen's University, physicist and recent winner of the Nobel Prize in physics for the earliest experiments proving the physical existence of neutrinos. Dates: 1 and 3

MacAllister and Queen's...both Scottish

Dr. Miles Oliver, physicist and senior lecturer at the University of London, Eng. Solar fusion expert, author of papers and textbooks on the standard solar model. On loan to Queen's Univ. for a year. Dates: all 3

He's miles from home...

Dr. Morgan Washington, graduate engineer from University of Alabama, on loan to the CNP project from the Univ. of Hawaii. Worked on a deep-sea neutrino detector off the coast of Hawaii; neutrino count came up short. Expert with photomultipliers under water. Dates: all 3

Washington and Hawaii...both are States...

Dr. Kelly Rowe, PhD in radiation physics, on faculty of Laurentian Univ. Responsible for shielding the project from background radiation and for screening out of the neutrino counts. Dates: all 3

Rowe and radiation...

Dr. Sam Carney of LBL, engineering architect of the geodesic dome used to support the photomultipliers. Flies to Sudbury frequently from Berkeley to oversee the reassembly and installation. Dates: all 3

34

Carney and California...

> *Dr. Hilaire Modeste, on loan to the CNP from CERN in Geneva, has done brilliant small-particle accelerator research on neutrinos. Resident at University of Guelph for two years. Dates: all 3*

Modest small particles...there's a stretch!

> *Dr. Harry Mintzman, "Mintz", has done original small particle theory at Columbia University in NY state. Believes neutrinos oscillate in mass and energy, and that the CNP will count them all and uphold the SSM. Dates: all 3*

"Mintz" from New York...

> *Zack Meyer, PhD in theoretical physics at McGill; thesis is on our CNP project's conception and results. Dates: Sept. 6th only*

Meyer and McGill...

> *Dr. Juan Hernandez, independent researcher with PhD in physics, old Mexican die-hard opposed to the standard solar model and to the very existence of neutrinos. Hates the millions of dollars being wasted on neutrino detectors. Writes anti-neutrino articles in the popular press and talked Siegel into giving him a hearing at the August workshop. Siegel gave in, hoping the guys could talk some sense into him. Dates: August 8th only*

Hernandez from Mexico...easy.

> *Also present, for the most part, were myself, Siegel, Alex, and Jack.*

Here ended the handwritten notes. A pretty distinctive crowd -- no wonder Siegel was looking for a quiet solution. Nell suddenly sensed she was in over her head; there was a damn good chance her mission would flop.

The telephone rang in the kitchen, Siegel calling from Ottawa.

"Have they got you in harness yet?"

"They didn't waste any time...I was just feeling a little daunted by the science team. Mike gave me his notes. Not much to go on, except the outstanding work they've all done."

"Just the bare bones, eh? That's Mike, when it comes to people, short and sweet. Have you got a pencil?"

"Yes."

"I want you to have some fllesh and blood background on these people...it helps to remember that scientists have feet of clay like everybody else."

"How timely! I'll be meeting everyone over drinks -- I could use some equalizing."

"Well here goes. First, we have Cam MacAllister at Queen's -- he's the head of the team. Mike probably told you he just got the Nobel Prize for work on neutrinos done back in the 50's in a mine shaft in Colorado. A thorough researcher, a fair and objective man, and an excellent chairman. I'd trust him with my life."

"Feet of clay, did you say?"

"Cam's feet are on solid ground, but he has his problems like everybody else. He's nearly 70 and his wife Nettie is in a nursing home with Alzheimer's. She was a sweet and pretty woman and now she doesn't even recognize him. The project keeps his mind off it."

"Poor man."

"Then we have Dr. Miles Oliver, from London, England. Well-known name -- writes and edits textbooks. Cuts quite a figure, too. I don't know him personally, but he's a damn fine lecturer and can hold an audience like no one else."

"Got that," said Nell, scribbling.

"Now we come to Dr. Juan Hernandez, an old Mexican fellow who challenged Einstein's theories and doesn't believe in neutrinos. He lives in Oregon now and has been writing some pretty convincing articles for the popular press. He thinks this whole neutrino hunt is a waste of money and even got himself onto the evening news. I flew him to one of our meetings to give him a hearing, but mostly to get the group to try to bring him

36

around."

"Could he be right?" asked Nell.

"Anything's possible, but the predictions of the Standard Model of particle physics, based on Einstein's formulas, have been borne out again and again by the accelerator tests. The Top Quark, until recently a prediction, has now been found. More pieces of the puzzle are fitting into place all the time. Current thinking says he's wrong, but who knows? In 50 years current thinking may put him above Einstein."

"Mike made more notes on him than on anyone else," commented Nell.

"Can't blame him...he's an outsider, a troublemaker for the project."

"Yes, but you wouldn't think someone so openly opposed to the project would be stupid enough to sabotage it. What about Dr. Morgan Washington? There's a name!"

"Dr. Washington has engineering experience in the underwater detection of neutrinos, off the coast of Hawaii -- that project, like all the others, came up short on the counts. He'll be resident here, to keep the photomultipliers and their panels aimed correctly. Initially, he'll be working under the direction of Sam Carney of LBL, who designed the assembly. Washington's a rather solemn fellow -- takes his work seriously, and he's quiet socially."

"What's LBL?"

"Lawrence Berkeley Laboratories, at Berkeley, California. A US Government lab. Lawrence was the chap who designed the first particle accelerator. Sam Carney is a design genius. He's been coming here regularly to check the installation of the photomultipliers -- their angles are calculated by computer, but set manually. Sam was here in August when the elevator panel was sacked and he called Cam in a real state about it. His family was with him on that trip to take a canoeing holiday. His boy Walter, about 15, had got in with some bad kids in California and done some pretty malicious vandalism. Sam got him into Outward Bound and thought the canoe trip might be good for him. He just assumed the kid had wrecked the elevator, which is why he called Cam."

"*Did* he wreck the elevator?"

"He swears he took the bus into town that afternoon but can't prove it. Nobody really knows."

"Wheels within wheels!"

"There's more to come. Dr. Moira Houston...but you'll meet her soon enough. I don't want to overload you. Call me after the social evening and we'll talk again when you've had a chance to put faces to names."

"Good to hear from you," replied Nell, replacing the receiver in its cradle, considerably cheered by the call.

CHAPTER 6

When Nell surfaced into consciousness too early on the dark Tuesday morning, a leaden weight of foreboding hung over her. Scheduled for today was the long descent into the underground mine; her unconscious mind was ill at ease. Nell cursed her old enemy, claustrophobia, and knowing she would have to prepare herself, left the warm bed for a head-clearing four-mile run on a frigid Sudbury morning. As she ran through unfamiliar suburbia, occasional snowflakes drifted silently under the five a.m. streetlights.

As always, the run dispelled any hint of physical or psychic tension, and she arrived back in the apartment fresh-faced and exhilarated, with time over to shower and breakfast heartily on Sonia's eggs -- brought in a flight bag from Galiano -- scrambled over a toasted poppyseed bagel. No coffee this morning, damn the shaft!

She arrived in the office an hour early to find Mike Bridges brooding over an electrical diagram. He checked his watch. "Good!" he declared over his glasses. "We've got time for a look at the project. Come on!"

Nell kept her coat on and followed Bridges outside the administration building, along a sidewalk through an area of broken, snow-covered rock, and into a large high-ceilinged warehouse full of boxes, cables, PVC pipe, and a forklift. In the middle of the warehouse stood the largest elevator Nell had ever seen, a strongly built metal cage the size of a small room, about six feet by twelve. Nell did not have time to worry about the trip down; the "cage" was ready and waiting for them. The doors rolled shut and the old lift lurched into its descent. A single bulb illuminated their surroundings as the platform dropped with surprising speed down the concrete shaft, dimly visible through the bars and shadows.

"It takes about three minutes," said Bridges. "We're travelling over a mile straight down through the Precambrian Shield -- through granite. We're doing about thirty miles an hour."

Nell's hands were buried deep in her coat pockets, fingernails pressed into palms that were slippery with sweat. Her heart was pounding and her eyes began to blur. "Take...deep...breaths!" she urged herself, sensing this weakness would be scored against her by Bridges, opposed to her appointment from the start.

She was on the edge of panic. Images of power blackouts and cave-ins loomed up, turning her knees to water. A black haze moved in, engulfing her consciousness. She squeezed her eyes shut and inwardly cried out, "Help me, God!" From somewhere across those black shores of terror came a thin filament of light, the light of reason, barely visible, but growing brighter. She opened her eyes and could focus again.

Her throat was dry. Leaning against the cage she looked around, trying to take an interest in the old lift, then swallowed in preparation for speech.

"What? No piped-in music for the troops?"

"The shaft was built for miners, not tourists," snapped Bridges, again on his short fuse. "Too noisy for music anyway. The cage is usually full of men and equipment."

The three minutes were taking forever, but at least Bridges seemed unaware of her ordeal. Two large concrete blocks on cables sped upwards in the shaft, one on either side.

"The halfway mark," said Bridges. "They counterbalance us." There was a sharp lurch and the light flickered momentarily. Nell, already white from strain, suppressed a gasp and stared hard at the tips of her winter boots, minutely examining the fine-grained leather, forcing her attention outward as reason flagged anew. Bridges was speaking.

"...you'll get used to that -- the cable's so long it slips on the drum a bit. There's a loose connection in the lighting somewhere -- don't worry, we have flashlights stashed in the box here," and he lifted the lid of a steel toolbox welded to the side of the cage. Inside were two long Magnum flashlights, a screwdriver kit, and a large adjustable wrench. He dropped the lid and the box snapped shut.

Nell became aware of a warm updraft and moved to loosen her scarf, still in place from the winter above.

"The earth is warm inside," explained Bridges. "The warm air rises through the shaft."

The elevator slowed abruptly, then bounced a little before coming to rest. A buzzer sounded and Bridges swung a mechanical lever to open the doors. "The doors are fail-safe. In case of a power failure, we can always get in and out of the lift -- and there's alternate power on top to pull up the cage."

"How do you talk to them?" asked Nell, sanity returning with the opening doors.

"There's an emergency telephone behind that little brass panel," he pointed, "and failing that, you push this buzzer five times as a signal to the top. It sounds everywhere. Someone'll come to operate the emergency hoist. The buzzer has battery-power backup."

They exited the lift onto a kind of loading dock, an expansive concrete apron upon which large crates were neatly piled. A forklift stood at the ready on the edge of the apron. Bridges crossed the platform and mounted a four-seater tram which sat waiting on the tracks. The diesel rattled to life and Nell was whisked off along a dimly lit hardrock tunnel, a footpath running along the left side, parallel to the tracks.

"This tram," explained Bridges, "and everything else you see down here that is more than ten feet long, had to be moved down in pieces and reassembled. That cage is the limiting factor."

The tunnel branched off into other dark orifices along the way; tracks entered each void in the rock face. "There are still some ore deposits down these old tunnels," motioned Bridges with a thumb, "but they quit mining this level a few years ago because of richer discoveries nearer the surface. It's a vast old mine, honeycombed with tunnels and old shafts -- not a place you'd want to get lost in."

The tunnel swerved abruptly to the left, the steel of new tracks glistening in the headlights. "This is where the access drift to the project leaves the main tunnel. From now on you won't see any more side tunnels."

The new track was smoother and the freshly excavated rock walls blacker than in the main line.

"We're into the norite now," continued Bridges. "It's ideal for the neutrino project -- it's low in radioactivity, and it's strong, good quality rock. There's a helluva lot of stress on a large cavity this deep in the earth."

Nell was growing more comfortable as they sped through the subterranean depths, with this capable man, rugged as the surrounding rock, narrating their journey.

He braked the tram as they passed on the left a steep tunnel with a sign over it, "Ramp to Lower Levels". A set of tracks disappeared into the darkness below. Moments later a vertical door marked "Observatory Entrance" appeared directly in front of them, a green light glowing in the darkness beside it. Bridges reached under the dash, entered a code on a remote control, and the door rolled upward into a rock slot; he then gunned the diesel along the tracks to another door which rose spontaneously and lowered behind them. Nell found herself in a brightly-lit automatic carwash station. She raised an arm to shield her eyes from the harsh fluorescence above.

"From this point onwards," he said, "we maintain cleanroom conditions. Incoming freight is all containerized, the containers are washed down with powerful jets of hot soapy water and rinsed. And you, young lady, are about to take a shower," as he led Nell along a corridor to the women's change-room.

"I had one about an hour ago," she objected.

"Sorry. Regulations. The laboratory area is scrupulously clean -- an absolute minimum of radioactive dust and particles. You'll find everything you need -- soap, towels, coveralls, and cap. Leave your purse in a locker and bring the key with you. See you in ten minutes," and with that he disappeared into the men's shower.

While washing away her own scented soap with the lab's institutional bar, Nell made a mental note not to shower at home on days that she would be going down the mine -- if they could be predicted. In a drawer she found sanitized coveralls sealed in plastic marked "Biz", which were too small, and several far too large pairs that were unmarked, obviously on loan from the men's room. She managed to get a pair of these on over her skirt, rolled up the sleeves and cuffs, donned an oversize cap, and caught a glimpse of herself looking like an understuffed scarecrow. More mental notes -- buy coveralls that fit, as Biz had done, and wear slacks to work -- and try to avoid the damn nightmare of coming down here in the first place!

When Nell emerged baggily from the change-room, Bridges, waiting in the hallway, erupted in laughter without making the slightest attempt to conceal his amusement. "On to the control room!" and he feigned to march.

Nell was irritated. Surely he could have mentioned the showering routine the day before. Perhaps not -- there was a competitive edge to their relationship. She spoke with icy precision. "Will I have to shell out for proper coveralls, or can the project afford a pair?"

Bridges laughed, seemingly oblivious. "Pick up a pair from Workwear World -- keep the receipt and pay it from petty cash."

They walked along the meticulous corridor, concrete walls and floor enamelled in a sparkling white, then arrived at a pair of swinging doors with eye-level windows and surrounding airtight flanges.

"This is the control room," said Bridges, sweeping the flanged door open for her. "It has its own clean-air system, not only for radioactivity, but as a refuge from fire."

"What if a fire starts in *here?"*

"Unlikely. It's pretty-well fireproof. The walls and floor are poured concrete, and the furniture's a hard flame-resistant plastic. There's very little paper around -- the operating manuals and the neutrino observations will all be stored on the computer network. The change-rooms are also fireproof."

Across the wide octagonal room stood Alex Wong, who raised a hand to her, then motioned to Bridges.

"Excuse me, Mrs. Fitzgerald, Alex needs a word. Have a look around." He flicked a switch and the cavity outside the windows of the control room lit up.

The place was extraordinary. It was like a big space station in the middle of the earth. She was standing upon a concrete octagon about sixty feet in diameter. The walls and ceiling formed a glass dome, the glass embedded in stout concrete ribs, which rose eight feet, then vaulted upward to follow the ceiling of the huge cavity, which extended about ten feet above the control room dome. The newly blasted-out cavity, illuminated with floodlight, was coated with enamelled concrete.

Two flanged doors on either side of the control room opened onto a ten-foot wide octagonal deck, which encircled the dome back as far as the igloo-like entrance through which they had come. Around the deck ran a protective railing at about waist height. Visible at intervals along the railing were the tops of vertical, shipboard-like ladders which hung over the side into the void beneath.

The control room itself was largely empty, save for a bank of computers around its far perimeter, and a control station off to the left, equipped with radio, telephone, and a complex array of levers, dials, and lights. In the middle of the octagonal floor was a circular hole, four feet across, surrounded by a rail, with a ladder protruding, as from the engine-room of a ship. As Nell advanced toward it, a slight young man in coveralls came hand-over-handing his way up the ladder, nodded hello, and trotted over to the telephone.

"Sig? That number three cable is binding -- could you take the weight off it? Gimme a couple 'a minutes," and he disappeared down the ladder to a lower deck.

Nell looked up to see Bridges returning.

"Okay, now for the guided tour. We haven't got long." He took Nell over to a computer and produced a "you-are-here" diagram of the entire excavation and the observatory within it.

"See, the deck that this dome sits on is just the tip of the iceberg -- this cavern is actually a hundred feet deep," and he motioned to the railing outside. "Anyone who falls over the edge there is toast. Below us they're working on the frame for the photomultipliers, and the acrylic tank inside that will hold the heavy water. Shorty over there, who just came up -- he runs the crane that hoists the pieces into position for the boys down below. This deck supports the ropes that will stabilize the tank, which'll hold a thousand tonnes of heavy water..."

"That's incredible!" exclaimed Nell. "Where are the supports for the deck itself?"

44

"There's a network of steel girders underneath -- they're cemented right into the norite. Come on, I'll show you."

He picked up a long Magnum flashlight and went out onto the deck, leaned over the rail, and shone the light down between the deck and the cavity wall. About six feet below the light struck a massive I-beam running out from under them into the rock face. He switched off the Magnum. A sliver of light was visible from the depths of the cavity. "That's coming from the assembly platform, right down at the bottom. When we've finished the construction, we'll be filling this whole cavity with ultrapure water -- almost up to the deck. The round acrylic tank that holds the heavy water will be almost floating in the ultrapure, so the ropes that stabilize it won't be bearing all that much weight."

He shone the light against the cavity wall. "The whole cavity has been shotcreted -- there's a machine that mixes cement and water as it sprays. After the shotcrete dried we sprayed nine coats of polyurethane over the whole cavity to make a waterproof liner. It'll keep out the radon gas, too, which would interfere with the signals."

"This is extraordinary!" marvelled Nell. "All because of a theoretical particle that may not even exist..."

"Hell, you've only seen the top!" boasted Bridges cheerfully. "We've just got time to go down the ramp. Back to the trolley now."

They retraced their steps past the change-rooms to the carwash and mounted the tram. He backed onto a side track to turn around, entered the remote control code for the observatory door, and once again they were out in the tunnel. Soon to their right appeared the descending tunnel she had seen earlier; he shifted to low and they plunged down the steep curving tracks which fell away into the depths.

"This is the steepest grade, leading down to the floor of the cavity. It's why we need diesel power on the tram."

The gloom of the ramp was punctuated by dim overhead lightbulbs; their headlights bounced shadows off the black rock. As before, a narrow footpath ran down beside the tracks. The ramp flattened out and they pulled up in front of another vertical door. Again Bridges entered a code and they drifted down a second incline to a landing, beyond which were two large solid metal doors. These rolled open to reveal a huge cavernous void that loomed upward into inky blackness.

The floor of the cavern consisted of a great octagonal platform whose corners were attached to cables running upwards into the void. Upon this stage the shadowy figures of seemingly miniature workmen could be seen at locally-illuminated assembly points; a welder here, a fitter there, a foreman with hardhat and clipboard en route. Beyond, a ghostly geometric mountain rose like a backdrop in the gloom.

"Spooky," whispered Nell, in awe.

"Not everybody's cup of tea," replied Bridges. "We've had a few chaps get into a real funk about the place and quit their jobs." He parked the tram just inside the doors and stepped over to a panel on the cavern wall. He picked up a mike and spoke into a loudspeaker.

"Bridges here. The floodlights will be on briefly for a demonstration." The amplified voice echoed eerily around the chasm above.

"Okay. We'll start at the top." He flicked a switch and four powerful floodlights midway up the cavern walls streamed white light into a massive sphere which was hanging under the control room deck.

"That's the top half of the acrylic globe which will hold the heavy water," he explained. "It's about forty feet across. It's made up of about a hundred curved plastic panels, all bonded together. The lower half is being assembled on this platform -- when it's complete, the upper one will be lowered and bonded to it."

Bridges touched another switch and an overhead floodlight beamed down onto the far side of the gigantic platform to reveal the lower bowl of clear acrylic, now about half assembled.

"We've still got 50 panels to go," said Bridges. "The plastic's about four inches thick so it's quite a job."

Nell was all but speechless. "Why this is a major, major project -- it's right up there with the Eiffel Tower, or the Golden Gate Bridge, or..."

"Now don't get carried away!" laughed Bridges. "Come over here and have a closer look."

He led the way across the platform to where the bonding was being done. The wall of the quarter sphere rose high into the air.

46

"Why, this part alone would hold a two-storey house!" she marvelled.

"At least that," said Bridges. "Now come around the back here and take a gander at the lower half of the geodesic dome."

At the far recess of the cavity, behind the plastic sphere, a hemispherical superstructure was under construction. Fitted to the stainless steel struts were triangular panels. Each panel held about twenty circular reflectors, each with a tube at its core, much like a flashlight bulb and reflector.

"These tubes are the eyes of the detector," spoke Bridges. "Each tube will be individually connected to the computer in the control room. The tubes must be precisely angled in order to pick up the neutrino signals coming from the tank."

"Yes, it does seem to have eyes," said Nell with a shudder. It resembled the head of some enormous all-seeing insect.

Bridges picked up a pair of binoculars and passed them to Nell. "Now look up to the top...see the top half of the geodesic dome?"

She adjusted the glasses and there came into focus a vivid picture of the clear acrylic dome, and through it, as through glass, the triangular web of seeing eyes mounted on the upper half of the great steel shell. Nell took a deep breath. "Incredible," she said softly, almost to herself. "Beyond belief."

She handed the glasses back to Bridges. "I'll do my best here," she said soberly, humbled in this moment by the enormity of the human quest for knowledge.

CHAPTER 7

When they arrived back in the office at 9:00, Bridges asked Jack Suhara to take Nell on a tour of the above-ground facility to prepare her for her part in hosting the guests, who would be arriving late the next day, Wednesday.

Jack led Nell along a footpath through the snow to a group of four large trailers, on loan from Laurentian University, which served as dormitories for the project. Each trailer contained six rather spartan units, equipped with single bed, bureau cum desktop, toilet, shower, and television. The rooms opened onto a long corridor with small windows which ran the length of the trailer, an exit door at either end.

Their next stop was the photomultiplier reassembly shop, which, like the laboratory, ran under cleanroom conditions, and could not be entered without the shower and change routine. Jack led Nell over to a window, through which she could see technicians at work, fitting the reflectors onto the triangular panels which would be boxed and lowered through the earth's crust to be fixed to the geodesic dome.

"Are those photomultipliers?" asked Nell, pointing to a high pile of solid wooden crates marked "Fragile" at the end of the workshop.

"Yes," he replied. "They are very delicate and must be handled with great care. There was an accident and some of the tubes were broken."

"Really? When did that happen?" she asked, playing the part.

"It happened early in September, during the lunch hour, before they started locking up at noon. The building was always

48

locked at night, but this was not considered a high security project -- not like a defense project. Now the doors are always locked."

"It may not have been an accident, then? How much do the crates weigh?"

"Oh, not too much. Seventy, eighty pounds, maybe."

A man or a woman could topple them, she thought.

"What about the technicians?" she asked. "Maybe someone has a grudge or something."

"I don't think so," replied Jack. "There is no sign of unrest in the workshop. These men and women are proud to be on the project. They are highly specialized technicians -- all the tubes must be tested by computer before they are fitted, at very precise angles, onto the dome panels. I don't think so."

The conversation ended rather abruptly as Jack turned and led the way back into the main administration building via a side entrance which led them through the cafeteria, then up in the elevator to the second floor, and into a meeting room with half a dozen office tables fitted together as a conference table. The room would seat about twenty people. On the same floor were two smaller meeting rooms, a lounge where the reception would be held, and a number of offices equipped with PC's for the use of visitors. This was an old building, explained Jack, which had been in use for many years as the central business and social facility for the old nickel mine.

Back in the office, Jack directed Nell to a file in her PC headed "Workshops".

"This is how Sue handled the arrangements for the scientists. There's a Sudbury chambermaid service which cleans the rooms and rents linen for the trailers. And you'll find notes on organizing the cafeteria staff for the reception and dinner."

"Not another hat!" she thought, hoping this added responsibility for a smooth-running reception would not interfere with the social role that she intended to play that evening.

♦

Wednesday dawned cold and overcast and by afternoon coffee a north wind was howling outside the old frame building and a lead sky hung over the project site. The physicists started to arrive in ones and twos; as each entered with briefcase in hand, buttoned, scarfed and hatted against the cold, a frigid gust of arctic air would whistle through the office. Bridges met the visitors in person, escorting them across the compound to their trailers, and by four-thirty a blinding snowstorm had moved in, punctuated by the cheerful shouts and greetings of the project colleagues, the office door banging to and fro, and the stomping and wiping of snow-clogged boots.

Nell had performed her duties well and everything was proceeding like clockwork when the guests began drifting into the reception lounge at 6:00. There was an air of conviviality bordering on revelry, such as often infects human gatherings when a sudden and dramatic change in the weather will act as an icebreaker.

The no-host bar was in good order over on the left of the spacious old maple-floored room, and Nell had just set up the evening's CD's, starting with some Stephane Grappelli, when she happened to glance up. Entering the room was a slender white-haired man with the most extraordinary presence she had ever seen. He stood for a moment in the doorway, looking about him, shirt open at the neck, holding his sportsjacket by the collar. In the simple act of thus just standing -- alert, quiet, and collected -- he reminded her of a wild animal, a deer perhaps, in the concentrated attention of listening for some distant forest sound.

When his gaze came around to Nell, his eyes rested briefly upon her, then his face came alight in a sudden smile, and he asked, "Did you have trouble with the snow?"

"I didn't have to deal with it," she replied, feeling awkward in the presence of such unusual grace. "That is, I work here, I'm not one of the scientists. I was here all day, working in the administration office." This rush of verbosity, this need to explain, was not like her, it made her feel lame. She reached up and brushed one of the long strands of hair away from her face.

The stranger's smile faded to an expression of repose, but his eyes held hers with a depth of observation she had never seen before. She felt herself to be in the presence of a god, a being who could penetrate the contents of the human mind and heart through receptivity alone. Then a quietness overtook her, a stillness, and all embarrassment receded. The strands of Mary

50

Magdalene's song stirred in her memory: "I don't know how to love him...I don't see why he moves me; he's a man, he's just a man..." "My *God*," she thought, "the song of the prostitute who loved Christ! What is going *on* here?" Embarrassment returned. Nell looked around and to some relief saw Bridges approaching, accompanied by a fair-haired man in his early thirties.

"Ah, there you are, Siddhu," spoke the younger man. "I dropped by your room to pick you up but you'd left. Please, I'd like you to meet our chief engineer, Mike Bridges. Mike, this is Siddhu Krishna, our speaker this evening."

"Glad to know you," drawled Bridges in his all-encompassing way. He extended a large male paw towards the slight hand of the East Indian who stood before him.

"Your project is fascinating!" exclaimed the older man in an educated voice. "But I have not been introduced to the young lady."

"Sorry, mate!" Bridges turned to Nell. "This is Mrs. Nell Fitzgerald -- she's helping out in the office. She set up the party for tonight. Nell, meet Dr. Robin Kettering from the UBC Department of Religious Studies."

"Robin," he said pleasantly, extending his hand. "I study Buddhism and cosmology -- the links between inner and outer space -- and I invited Siddhu to our dinner tonight to speak about inner space."

Nell shook hands with Robin. He too was a rather striking man, finely built, tallish. She turned to Siddhu, who bowed slightly as he shook her hand, then made the lovely *namaste* gesture over two facing palms. The sculptured face had an air of reverence.

Nell held the eyes of the old man until he smiled acknowledgement of the introduction, then glanced at Bridges, who wore a guarded scepticism. Yes, you could have expected that.

Three people in high spirits entered the room, amidst calls of "Where's the grog?" and "Help, antifreeze! My veins are slush!" Bridges called out, "Hi Sam! Help yourself to anything, you old Yankee dog!" and moved away to join the merriment.

"Is there anything I could get you from the bar, Mrs. Fitzgerald? Siddhu?" asked Robin.

"I'd like a glass of white wine, please," she replied to Robin, but the man of grace quickly insisted on getting the drinks for all three of them. He returned a few moments later with two glasses of white wine and a tumbler of mineral water for himself.

Nell addressed herself to Siddhu. "What is inner space, Mr. Krishna?"

"Inner space is the universe of consciousness that each one of us carries within. There are about six billion different inner spaces alive on the planet -- and that's just the humans!"

"Yes, I see -- we are all different," she said. "But what is the point of studying that?"

"Ah, you do not wish me to give my speech twice, do you?" the old man answered with a twinkle.

"Oh, no!" Nell replied quickly. "It just sounded intriguing," and looked to Robin for help.

"Siddhu and I have a lot in common," interjected Robin. "We begin by agreeing that the study of space and the particles within it is not important unless it has a bearing on our welfare and the quality of our lives."

"That is true," accorded Siddhu. "Our quest to understand the universe must support our correct and proper place within it."

A clean-shaven, rather dapper man had eased up to the group. "Our place within the universe is to occupy a random moment in geologic time," he stated, bypassing introductions, "on a planet which will grow cold when the sun has burned out."

Robin stepped in. "Oh hullo, Sidney. Have you met Mrs. Fitzgerald? She's working with Mike. Mrs. Fitzgerald, this is Dr. Sidney Hawthorpe, Department of Physics, Penn State. And to your left, Sidney, is our dinner speaker, a good friend of mine, Siddhu Krishna."

"Are you a philosopher, Mr. Krishna?" asked the rather prim-faced, bespectacled Hawthorpe.

"Sir," replied Siddhu quietly, "I am a student of human consciousness," and he gave an enquiring look to Nell and motioned towards her glass. She passed it to him for a refill as he slid away from his inquisitor.

"Who is this friend of yours?" Hawthorpe asked Robin. "Is he here to enlighten us?" and it was clear that Hawthorpe felt himself enlightened enough already.

"Excuse me, Sidney," said Robin, "but I must take Siddhu around to meet the others. Would you look after Mrs. Fitzgerald, please?" and with a wink at Nell he ducked away.

"What is your specialty in physics?" Nell asked dutifully.

Hawthorpe hesitated, seemingly taken aback that anyone would not know who he was. "I'm a full professor in the Astrophysics Department. I'm working towards a grand unification theory that will explain all the laws of nature in one coherent framework."

A very tidy man, thought Nell. He wants a tidy universe.

"Kind of a theory of everything?" she asked sweetly.

Hawthorpe frowned and made a quick gesture of irritation. "Hardly a theory of *everything!*" he snapped. "Of course that's not possible. My work involves the forces of the universe, and the evolution and future of matter. Much of the puzzle has already been solved, and soon we will have full control of the situation. And may I ask what brings you to our reception?"

"Oh, I'm just a here and now secretary," she smiled. "I get to look after the dinner arrangements -- and that reminds me -- if you'll excuse me I must see if the situation is under control in the kitchen," and smiling to herself she headed out of the lounge.

The baron of beef was on schedule, ready in twenty minutes. It was to be a smorgasbord dinner, with pesto linguini as an alternate, Waldorf salad, and trifle for desert.

Nell returned to the lounge, entering just behind a rather elegant woman of about forty in a sleek black dress. She held her head high and scanned the room expectantly, then spotted Bridges and made a beeline for him, sweeping without a glance past Biz and another woman who had turned to acknowledge her.

"Hello Michael! What ghastly weather you've put on for us! How *are* you my dear?" and she flashed him a dazzling smile over her decolletage.

It wasn't clear from Bridges' expression how he felt about this striking creature, but Nell found herself curiously intent.

Bridges moved one step backwards and replied, amicably enough, "Things are running more or less on schedule, Moira, but I don't seem to have much drag with the weatherman in these parts. Now down in Melbourne, that was a different story!"

"I bet it was!" she winked invitingly. "I've seen pictures of those crowded beaches, full of brawn and beauty!" And she actually reached over and touched her fingertips to the mat of black hair above his open collar. He grinned, then, in mock seriousness, "Moira -- behave yourself!"

Nell wondered for the first time if Bridges was married. He seemed comfortable enough with this woman so perhaps it was just a friendly flirtation.

Nell approached Biz and the other woman that Moira had casually snubbed and stopped by to say hello.

"Hi Nell!" said Biz warmly. "This is a great party! Have you met Kelly? This is Dr. Kelly Rowe from Laurentian University. She's our background radiation whiz."

Nell shook hands with a perky, compact woman in her late forties.

"What I do," said Dr. Rowe in a matter-of-fact way, "is to get the computers to ignore the stuff we don't want to count -- nothing too glamourous about that!"

"Don't believe her for a minute!" said Biz. "She's got one of the toughest jobs on the project, you can take it from me -- computers are my business! That's why they've got her resident here in Sudbury."

Kelly turned to Nell. "What's your line around here?"

"I seem to be something of a gopher -- I'm filling in for Sue in Mike's office while she's on mat leave."

"She's only been here a couple of days and she's practically running the place," chimed Bix. "Mike's in a better mood already."

"Who's the lady in black?" asked Nell lightly.

Both women glanced discreetly at Bridges, then back at Nell.

Kelly spoke first. "That's Moira Houston. Supernova expert. She's brilliant. I don't know if she's really after Mike or not, maybe she's just playing. He's kind of hard to read, too."

Biz spoke up. "Mike doesn't wear a ring, he doesn't like rings, but he has a wife in Toronto and two kids at U of T. He flies home the weekends that he can get out of here. You can see that he has to fend them off, can't you?" And Nell had to agree that he did have a certain animal magnetism.

She watched as Moira squeezed Mike's arm with another fetching smile and then turned in their direction.

"How are the computer techies?" she threw over her shoulder, en route to the bar.

Biz and Kelly muttered minimal greetings and turned back to Nell.

"She doesn't talk to our level much, or our sex," explained Biz.

"Did you know her husband committed suicide?" asked Kelly.

"No!" exhaled Biz. "Where did you hear that?"

"Overheard it at a meeting," said Kelly. "And she has this genius reclusive son that she never talks about."

"How unlikely she seems as a physicist," marvelled Nell aloud, and made a mental note to follow up on Siegel's unfinished remark of Monday night.

"She's very serious about her work," countered Kelly. "And much respected for it -- so she can get away with murder, socially, which she does!"

"I'd lay odds Mike plays it straight," said Biz. "He's got a nice wife."

Nell was keeping an eye on the room while they spoke together. Two men were coming along the hallway, heads bent in concentration, the shorter, younger man speaking earnestly to the older. Both stopped just inside the doorway, oblivious to the party around them.

Biz followed Nell's glance and said, "The man talking is Dr. Harry Mintzman from Columbia. He and Dr. Hoffman from UCLA are both in more or less the same camp in the neutrino debate -- they figure the counts keeps coming up short because the three sizes of neutrinos are oscillating back and forth, and that so far the equipment hasn't been sensitive enough to intercept them all."

Dr. Mintzman, a small wiry man, was speaking emphatically, gesturing with his hands, his face eager. The older man, Hoffman, smoked a curved pipe and wore a shaggy loose-fitting suit. Under the headful of grey hair was a face lined with kindliness. He now stood slightly stooped, leaning forward to hear, in a posture that through the years had become a hallmark at UCLA. Hoffman listened intently until Mintzman had finished, then began to speak in a low, resonant, unhurried voice that carried easily across to them.

"Either way, Harry, whether they are oscillating or not, so far we've only been able to count the electrons, not the muons or the taus. Once we can count all three, the tally should be about right."

"Those are the three types of neutrinos," explained Kelly to Nell. "And that will be part of my job, to identify them separately on the computers. The low-energy tau and muon neutrinos are going to be interesting little devils to count."

Nell was somewhat relieved to see the chef appear briefly in the hallway to motion the thumbs-up, meaning that the dinner would appear in ten minutes. She excused herself to relay this information to Bridges, who then announced that the guests should make themselves comfortable at the dinner table, have a glass of wine and a salad, the main course would arrive presently.

Nell waited until most of the guests were seated, then took her place beside a stockily-built moustached black man, who was sitting apart on his own. He smiled politely if not a little apologetically, nodded, and took some time unfolding his napkin. Nell leaned toward him, introduced herself, and asked if he had come a long way for the meeting.

"Oh, not that far, ma'am, only from Kingston. Ah'm Morgan Washington. I'm a consulting engineer, on loan to you folks from Hawaii."

"Oh yes, I heard there was an underwater project down there."

"That's right. I was on that," he said simply, taking a fork to his salad.

Dr. Washington spoke in the soft rhythmic tones of the South, but obviously he was not inclined towards much chat this evening. That was fine; it would give her a few moments to enjoy the fresh salad and a welcome lapse into her own thoughts.

CHAPTER 8

"Ah'm sorry, Mrs. Fitzgerald, I know I'm not being very communicative this evening. It's just that I've been worried about my work lately, and about some other things, too, of a personal nature."

"Oh, please don't mention it," said Nell. "No one should have to talk just for the sake of talking. I was enjoying a quiet moment myself!"

"Well, Ah've had a little *too much* quiet lately -- my marriage has broken up, down in Hawaii, which is mostly why I accepted this contract. But I miss ma children and ma missus too, even though she ran out on me."

"Oh, I am sorry!" said Nell. "I do understand -- I lost my husband in a skiing accident on the West Coast. I came here to try to put the past behind me." The lies she was telling to console this man were oddly disorienting.

Perhaps because of their mutual loss, Dr. Washington led into another subject that was on his mind. "I saw you at your desk, over beside Mike's office. Do you see much of Jack Suhara?"

"Not so far," replied Nell. "I've only been here a couple of days. He's taken me around to meet people and see the place a bit. Why do you ask?"

"Well, ma'am, we are both engineers and I've known Jack for some time. It's a small world, chasing neutrinos. He was on the Kuchino project and I'm not just sure how he feels about this project here in Canada. Perhaps I'm speaking out of turn, but he

57

felt he lost face in Japan when Kuchino didn't get the solar neutrinos they wanted, and some say he left Japan because of it. And now this Canadian project has been running late, and it worries me."

Nell remembered how stiffly Jack Suhara had reacted to Bridges on a couple of occasions; she had put it down to Bridges' bulldozer manner and cultural insensitivity.

"What are you saying?" asked Nell. "That he would interfere with this project because his own failed?"

"Well, he was chief engineer over there and he *feels* he failed. The theoretical folks see the solar neutrino problem as a kind of puzzle, or mystery, but he was *real close* to it, running the construction and all. On this new project he's just second fiddle, and maybe he don' *want* to be bettered. It sure would explain the delays I bin hearin' about..."

Washington Morgan was almost musing to himself. "But that's probably all wrong -- forget it, it's only a thought, and I've had a lot of time to think lately. I guess I'm just *para*noid!" and he smiled. "Let's go round up some of that beef."

As they pushed back their chairs, Nell heard a little gasp from Dr. Washington. His gaze was rivetted on a wraithlike creature, standing uncertainly in the doorway like an apparition from another epoch. The pale, straight, shoulder-length hair framed a long porcelain face with china blue eyes. Dressed casually in flowing pastel robes, she gave the impression of supple liquidity.

Dr. Washington's hand trembled slightly on the back of his chair. He said nothing more as they walked to the buffet, but his attention was fixed upon the young woman, who glided to a table and took a seat next to Robin Kettering, whom she greeted by name. Nell could not hear Robin's reply. She wanted to ask who the lady was but did not wish to further stress Dr. Washington.

Ahead of them in the buffet line-up could be heard a cultivated English voice which somehow gave the impression of silver. Nell peered around a tall man directly in front of her to catch sight of its source. The owner of the voice was standing easily in line, deliberating upon the state of the monarchy in Britain. He was a man of erect posture, slightly over average height, with a fine head of silver hair. He suddenly caught her eye with his own pale blue ones and nodded agreeably without breaking his train of thought. There was no doubt that this was the distinguished lecturer, Dr. Miles Oliver, whom Siegel had described to her on the telephone Monday night.

The tall man directly ahead of her had followed the glance of the Englishman and turned to face Nell.

"...and so that, in a nutshell, is how informed Londoners, who should know better, are reacting to our sadly tarnished throne."

The tall man looked back to the Englishman and replied, "What a pity," then turned back to Nell. "I don't believe we've met -- I'm Cam MacAllister from Queen's, and this gentleman is Dr. Miles Oliver, whom we are fortunate to have on sabbatical from the University of London. Miles is tops in solar physics."

Nell introduced herself once again, then found herself uttering the incredible words, "I'm very curious about solar neutrinos," to which Miles Oliver replied that he would be most delighted if she would allow him to give her a crash course over dinner.

Back at the table, Nell sat between Morgan Washington, who had again lapsed into silence, and Miles Oliver. Further along, Jack Suhara was talking to Moira. Bridges was with Cam MacAllister and Sam Carney. Robin, Siddhu, and the porcelain woman were digging into their pasta.

"Now dear lady," began Miles Oliver, "tell me what you know already, and we'll start from there."

"Horseradish?" asked Nell, stalling, her mind racing to remember anything at all, then seizing on what she had heard just ten minutes earlier. "There are three kinds, and sometimes they oscillate back and forth from one kind to another."

"Oscillation is not a certainty," remarked Oliver amiably, as he deftly carved off a piece of rare roast beef and dipped it in the juice.

"It might be wise to start at the beginning, with what is actually known," he went on. "That approach has proved best in the lecture-hall and has made my astronomy textbook series the standard throughout the world."

"I had no idea," said Nell pleasantly, as she savoured a mouthful of exquisitely tender beef. The dinner, thank heaven, was a success.

"To begin with then, the first thing we know to be true is how the sun burns at its core..." The words spilled out of him like jewels from a chest, elegantly and effortlessly, the silver oration music to the ear.

When everyone had finished their trifle and coffee, the dinner tables were moved to one end of the room, and the chairs were positioned in a semi-circle around a low platform which held a single chair. Presently the dinner guests took seats, and the speaker for the evening mounted the platform and sat very still in his own chair. For a moment he surveyed the group, waiting for silence to fall.

"Tonight we are going to examine the nature of knowledge, which is symbol, and to explore the possibility of going beyond symbol to a more direct perception of what truth is.

"Every one of us has our own universe of consciousness -- our unique past experiences, our present thoughts, beliefs, emotions, hopes, points of view. Even now, as you sit listening to a stranger, you may all seem to be having the same experience, but in fact each one of you is seeing the speaker from a different angle, both in your physical position in the room, and in the unique way you react to him. No two people here are having the same inner experience.

"If this is seen to be actually true in a deep way, it is disturbing to realize that we are very alone in the world, that we came into the world alone and will leave it alone and that our progress through it is a unique and solitary one.

"So to make our lives more comfortable and supported and less alone, we group ourselves into communities and friendships based upon common interest and agreement. This masks the underlying fact that we are separate and alone in ourselves. The point is illustrated by the ultimate punishment we reserve for the criminal, which is to place him in solitary confinement, where it is not possible to alleviate this underlying isolation..."

This was proving altogether too much for Sidney Hawthorpe. He suddenly called out to the room in general, "What has all this got to do with the neutrino project?"

"Please, sir, I am coming to that. Please be patient," said the speaker. "Does it disturb you to remember that you are alone?

"Now, may I describe each one of us as a mobile universe of experience? Each one of us wakes up in our own room, has our own clothes closet, kitchen, our own model of car, our own family and friends, our work -- in short, our own world. And the outside world mirrors our inner world every day, thus confirming it..."

"We are not six-year-olds!" snapped Hawthorpe. "Remember your audience!"

"I am speaking to men and women of great knowledge," replied Krishna. "Please just listen to what is being said.

"So we have on this planet a number of billion separate and different, yet experienced and confirmed, views of the world.

"So the question arises, are we able to experience any truth or perception which is not limited by our particular point of view? Are we capable of experiencing an absolute truth or perception which is the same for everybody?"

Miles Oliver's melodious voice opened up. "There is no way to prove or disprove this question so it is not a worthwhile subject for investigation."

"But you could say the same for particle physics," replied Krishna, "with the uncertainty principle of Heisenberg, which of course you already know. You cannot observe the position and the momentum of a particle at the same time. The very act of 'looking' at a particle, with gamma rays, changes its behaviour. You agree, sir?"

"I'm listening," nodded Oliver.

"So to continue, our framework for looking at the world, which is our growing knowledge, is always relative to the observer. The picture that we have built up as knowledge of the world is unique to ourselves and does indeed work for us and as a result we have become very attached to it. In fact this totality of what we have experienced in our own histories is what we identify *as* ourselves, and we each have a name for that, and when we die that name goes on a tombstone.

"So the question is, can we see the world today without influencing what we see now by the past world experiences we have stored in our memories and which make us unique? Can we see the world without that filter? Can the observer disappear and only the observed be present?"

Nell suddenly felt a thunderbolt of recognition: it jumped into her mind and just as suddenly was gone. She reached inwardly for it but it eluded her. And then she remembered her feeling of transparency under the receptive gaze of Krishna.

He was still talking. "If only the observed is present to consciousness, there can be only one truth. That is why knowledge is symbol. Knowledge is always old truth. It is symbol and it sets limitations on the mind. It obscures the view of new truth, of today's observerless reality."

Krishna surveyed the faces in the group, then pulled out a pocket watch and glanced at it.

"We have all had a long day...perhaps we can continue with this investigation later?"

Sidney Hawthorpe spoke up for a third time. "Can you not get to the point now, and relate all this to the neutrino?"

"It will take some time to reach that point, sir. We will go into it next time we meet. Thank you for your patience." And he stood up and walked out of the dining hall.

There was a general stir in the room as people's attention turned to one another. Nell glanced around to see what effect this unusual speaker had had. Robin Kettering wore a delighted smile and was also looking around; then he stretched his arms in the air and indulged himself in a happy yawn.

Mintzberg and Hoffman scraped their chairs back and left the room, heads bowed together in concentration as before, this hiatus in their own thoughts already forgotten. Cam MacAllister was sitting thoughtfully in his chair, working on the implications of what had been said. Morgan Washington had sat politely through the talk but it was doubtful to Nell that he had really listened. She caught a partial sentence, "...not going to sit through another bout of that crap" from Hawthorpe, and Miles Oliver wore an expression of benign tolerance towards this new-age poppycock from the colonies.

Biz came over to Nell and said she'd been talking to Bridges about the road conditions outside. The snow had been falling steadily throughout the evening and was now about a foot deep. Biz, Kelly, and Alex Wong were going to split the cost of a cab rather than attempt to drive to their respective homes. Nell lived out of the way and asked Bridges if she could use one of the spare beds in the dorm, rather than face the drive home after the long day.

"No problem," he said. "I sometimes stay here myself -- I've got a couch in back of my office. But mind, the compound will be locked so you'll be stuck here until morning."

It was freezing cold in the trailer; she turned up the electric heat. Nell had taken some salt from the dining room and managed to do a fair job of cleaning her teeth with a toothpick and a hot-water gargle. She got into the frigid bed fully dressed in order to warm it up, and turned off the light to think. She must have dozed off, for when she came to again, the room was warm and the echo of some small noise was lingering in her ears.

She waited, resisting the temptation to turn on the light and look at her watch. She sat up in bed and held the watch up to a sliver of light from the compound which shone through the curtains: 12:02 a.m. She lay back against the single pillow, and there it was again, a little creaking in the corridor outside. The walls were like paper. Then came a quiet rasp from the outside screen door.

Nell sat up to the window again, more careful this time not to be seen. A square, stockily built figure in a heavy overcoat and a fedora was slowly making its way across the compound towards the administration offices. It paused at the photomultiplier reassembly shop, then approached the door and tried the handle, which did not yield. Then the door to the shop opened from within, and the figure disappeared inside.

Nell decided to investigate. Around her coat she wrapped a white blanket to make her less conspicuous, should any wakeful soul glance out into the snowy, lighted compound.

The night watchman was on duty but was evidently indoors at the moment. Bridges had said that in cold weather he would do occasional walkabout, checking locks and the project elevator in the warehouse, and then return to his room to warm up. In his amblings about the site he would turn lights on and off around the compound to create an impression of nocturnal activity.

Nell eased herself out of the trailer into the crisp night air. It was clear now, and much colder. She assumed the role of insomniac, the sleepless widow stepping out for a breath of fresh air, and wandered about a little, yawning her way towards the reassembly shop. There was not a soul in sight nor a light showing from any of the dorms or the administration building,

63

where Bridges could well be sleeping.

When she reached the workshop, she crouched down below window level and worked her way along the side of the building until she found a window with a snow-covered shrub beneath it. There was just room to kneel, more or less out of sight, and listen. From the darkness within a man and woman were talking.

Nell reached into her pocket and pulled out the inner cardboard cylinder she had thought to remove from the toilet roll in the bathroom. With some difficulty she balanced herself so that she could place one end of the roll against the window and the other to her ear. The effect was startling -- a guttural male voice sounded clearly in the frozen silence of the winter night.

"...and the 1987 supernova is why it is inevitable that the solar counts will come up short."

"I cannot agree. The 1987 supernova proved exactly the opposite. If he keeps listening to you, he's going to be in serious trouble, personally and financially." Moira's voice was unmistakable -- and desperate.

"He listens to me intelligently, and I need his confidence and support. His new game will get the truth out to the whole world," argued the fedora.

"You could at least try to persuade him to postpone marketing the game until some of the counts are in," urged Moira. "It's only a matter of weeks!"

"I cannot do that," answered the man. "He wants the game to come out ahead of the counts -- he wants to be first to publicly expose this farce."

"It's a disaster either way," said Moira miserably. "If I'm right, he's wrong, and you're the cause of it! Well, at least these delays we're having will give me more time to talk sense into him..."

At that moment Nell heard one of the trailer screen doors rasp open and snap shut. She quietly flattened herself into the snow, thankful for the white blanket. Praying that the footprints leading to her window would not be noticed, she held her breath.

Footsteps crunched towards the workshop, but the shadow of the night watchman preceded him, obscuring Nell's prints. He mounted the steps, tried the door. Silence from within. His flashlight beam swept the boxes of photomultiplier tubes high at the back of the shop. Then, satisfied, the guard switched off his light and headed off towards the warehouse.

No sooner had the guard entered the warehouse than the workshop door opened, Moira emerged and walked with hurried steps back to her trailer. When Moira was out of sight, the workshop door opened again and the square man in the fedora tread carefully -- as if wary of slipping -- but in a composed and dignified manner, towards one of the other trailers.

Nell pondered what to do. Her hands burned with cold. How long would the guard be out of sight? She did not have long to think about it. He emerged promptly from the warehouse and trudged over to the administration building, where, instead of simply trying the door, he unlocked it, opened it, entered, and switched on a light. A few moments later the cafeteria light went on.

"Coffee!" whispered Nell triumphantly, and crept forward along the wall of the workshop. A thought struck her. She lay back at intervals, and arcing her arms over her head made the snow-angels of childhood, which would -- ?? -- signal the antics of some escaped lunatic? evince the wanderings of some errant nocturnal youth? or draw yet further attention to the footprints? No -- all sign of them had been erased. She looked back on this artwork with satisfaction, then set about replicating it at various points about the compound. Best to confuse the scent!

Nell was shivering when she finally got back into what now seemed a very warm room, and once safely in bed held up her watch to the window again: it was 12:16. The whole episode had taken less than fifteen minutes.

The light was still on in the administration building. Nell opened her window a crack so she could hear the guard come out, and watch him discover the snow-angels.

She curled up and tried to think. Who was this newcomer, and why was Moira meeting him so late at night? How had she gained access to the photomultiplier shop? And who was this "him" she was trying to protect? More important, would they try to sabotage the project, and if so, tonight?

Not likely, she decided. They'd had their chance. If she alerted Bridges, or the guard, the police would be called in. Nell's job was to watch and listen and report to Siegel. She would call him first thing.

A faint sound drifted across the frozen compound and Nell raised herself onto her elbows to watch the commissionaire stodgily making his way back to his trailer, halting here, stooping there, to examine the symmetrical, sparkling snow-angels which had magically appeared during his graveyard coffee break. Shaking his head in wonderment, he could be heard muttering under his breath, "I always knew they was crazy, but this one takes the cake."

CHAPTER 9

Nell awoke with a start at daybreak Thursday morning and looked anxiously at her watch. 6:58. She had a quick wash and donned the sage-green wool dress she had worn the day before -- not too much the worse for wear after its late night services to physics.

Entering the administration building she followed the aroma of bacon and coffee to the cafeteria, and glanced out into the parking lot. Bridges' old Bronco was not in the lot; he must have gone home for the night. She poured coffee and went to her office telephone. With any luck Siegel would still be at home.

He picked it up on the first ring. "Siegel."

"It's Nell. Got a minute?"

"What's up?" he asked quickly.

"I need to know more about Moira Houston," she replied. "She was out after midnight in the photomultiplier shop, talking to an old man I've never seen before. I didn't hear much of it, but they were talking about the 1987 super...super..."

"Supernova..."

"...supernova, and neutrino counts, and delays in the project."

"Good God!" whispered Siegel. "Did they *do* anything?"

"Not as far as I could tell. They were arguing over someone else -- someone who's selling a game. If the counts are high it will be bad for the game. Moira wants the game delayed until the counts come in. The old man wants the game to go ahead now -- to expose the farce, I think he said. Then the night watchman came along and shone his light onto the boxes above them and that broke it up. They both went to their rooms."

"Did you get a look at the old fellow?"

"From behind. Square and stocky, kind of European looking. Deep voice -- foreign accent, I think."

"Sounds like Hernandez, our anti-neutrino crank," reflected Siegel. "Did he wear a fedora?"

"Yes! I didn't realize he was here!"

"That's him, all right. Hmmm...even Hernandez has a stake in this thing," he thought out loud. "But it's a different stake from Moira's, I would have thought. I'm going to make some calls. Can you keep an eye on them today?"

"She'll be in meetings most of the day, and he'll be doing a presentation this afternoon. Tonight if there's not another blizzard they're going to bus everybody into Sudbury for a night on the town."

"Good. I'll get back to you as soon as I can."

"There's something else," Nell said doubtfully. "Morgan Washington. He's worried about Jack Suhara -- that maybe Jack doesn't want our project to succeed where the Japanese one failed..."

"That could saw both ways," Siegel put in quickly. "Washington's neutrino count was low, too. But if Jack is involved it's serious -- he has full access to everything. Look, you're in the office with him -- tell him you're interested in travelling to Japan or something. Get him talking. If there's any clue you might pick it up."

"I'll ask him for coffee this morning. It's hard to believe Dr. Washington would be involved -- he seemed so concerned for the project. But perhaps he's just depressed about his wife leaving him, and his judgement's off."

"I'm sorry to hear that. Yes, we only see the tip of the iceberg here at work. Is there anything else?"

"Isn't that enough!"

"More than enough. Listen, Mrs. Fitzgerald -- this is a little delicate. It's a particularly busy time for Mike, and I don't want him preoccupied with this problem. What you're getting into could be convoluted and I want you to report what you discover directly to me. Just watch things discreetly and don't bother him unless you see danger at hand. Understood?"

68

"Yes. That makes it easier. By the way, with the snowstorm last night I stayed in the dorm. I'd like to move in there for the week. It's plausible enough -- I'm the social convenor, and there's more snow on the way."

"Fine, so long as I can reach you," said Siegel.

"There's a cell phone in the office. I'll keep it with me," and they rang off.

With sudden alarm she wondered where Hernandez was this morning. Though he had been on the site for only one of the accidents, he seemed to be in some sort of collusion with Moira, who wanted the project delayed. Better ask Mike when he comes in.

She turned to yesterday's paper, from which she had been preparing a list of downtown entertainments for the guests. She was just printing the list when Bridges came stomping into the office in a state of high amusement over the snow-angels.

"Bloody hell! I can't *believe* anyone around here would do that! Old Harry didn't see anything, but he's sure shaking his head over it!" Then he looked at Nell. "It wasn't you, was it?"

Nell ignored the question and assumed her most withering look.

"A bloke can ask, can't he?"

"Will you be sitting in on the planning sessions this morning, sir?"

"Yes."

"Would you mind handing these out, then? I'll collect them later and after lunch I'll book the restaurants people want."

"Great," said Bridges. "How did you sleep?"

"Cold at first, but okay."

"Good. Now we're slated to have old Hernandez do his piece at 1:30 in the conference room. I'd like you to come and tape it."

"Be happy to. When does he arrive?" she asked innocently.

"Oh, he came in last night, after dinner. Tired, didn't want any speeches. I think he just hit the sack."

"He'll be at loose ends this morning then?"

"No, he was going into Science North for the morning, so don't worry about him. He's just here for today."

"How about Jack? Will he be in the meeting with you?"

"No, he'll be running things out here."

"He's very formal, isn't he?"

"He's a Jap! That's how they are. Damn fine engineer, though." He went into his office.

Nell followed him. "Speaking of engineers, I was talking to Dr. Washington over dinner."

"Phototubes under water, that's his line. Real serious about his work. Quiet fella, don't get to know him much."

As Siegel had said, Bridges wasn't much of a people man.

"Will Jack be going down to the observatory today?" she asked.

"Probably, the crew is down there laying the water pipe along the tracks."

"Could I go with him? I'd like to nose around a bit."

Bridges looked surprised. "I had an idea you weren't too keen on going down," he said easily.

Perhaps he wasn't such a fool.

"I'm not, but knowing there's an emergency hoist helps. And I've got to get used to it."

"Okay. Call-forward the phones to Mrs. Higgins if you go. She can ring down to Jack, or get me out of the meeting if necessary," and he headed for the conference room.

Jack had accepted Nell's offer of an early coffee before going down to check on the pipe-laying. They were alone in the cafeteria.

"I have a friend who went to Japan to teach English," remembered Nell. "She just loves it there!"

"Very different," said Jack. "Very crowded. But most people have work."

"Do you miss it?"

"Oh yes," he replied, then thinking better, added, "but here is good too -- except for the snow!"

"Was your project much like this one?"

"Yes, a long way down in the earth. And much farther from the city. But not so cold!"

How was she going to get him off the weather?

"What is a supernova?" she asked.

Jack suddenly brightened. "It's a massive ancient star that has burned up all the fuel at its core. It collapses, and then explodes,

70

very brightly. Sometimes, very rarely, we can see them with the naked eye -- maybe three in a century. The last one was in 1987."

"1987? I didn't see it."

Suhara laughed. "It could only be seen in the southern skies. It was recorded by a telescope in Chile. It also registered on two underground detectors -- both showed a neutrino flux about the same time."

"I thought neutrinos came from the sun."

"Some do. They come from many places," and he looked at his watch.

Wrong tack!

"So bits of the exploding star actually came through the earth?"

"Yes. Neutrinos are particles. They travel at the speed of light, so they were counted by our detector at exactly the same time the explosion was seen at ground level."

"Counted by *your* detector! How exciting!"

Jack's eyes glowed momentarily. "Yes, and the star was 170,000 light years away -- and that's close, for a supernova." Then his smile faded. "But our detector cannot count the sun's neutrinos, and the sun is only nine light minutes away. It is a big problem." He finished his tea and rose from the chair. "We must go to the mine now."

"This is fascinating!" she pursued, as they stepped out into the snow. "I'd love to know more about that supernova, and stars exploding. I wonder if the library..."

"You don't have to go to the library. We have one of the world's supernova experts right here -- Dr. Houston."

"Oh, the lady in black!"

"Do not be fooled by Dr. Houston's appearance. She is a brilliant physicist. Last night, after dinner, she spent hours in the workshop, going over the engineering drawings of the photomultiplier settings. The settings will record the angles of the neutrinos that pass through the detector. If another supernova explodes, she will know where it is in the sky and be able to count its neutrinos."

Nell paused to remember if Moira had been at the after-dinner speech...no, she had not.

"She must have missed Siddhu's talk," she observed casually.

71

"Oh yes. She went over right after dinner. I let her into the shop myself," and they stepped into the old lift, Nell's heart sinking in spite of her optimism that it would get easier.

"Go with it!" she told herself. "Heart, pound as hard as you like!" The self-talk helped, displaced the panic. Heart racing, adrenaline flooding her system, she was still in control.

She managed to think. Somehow, Moira and Hernandez had met and arranged the rendezvous during the course of the evening. Or had it been prearranged? If so, couldn't the matter have been discussed on the telephone? One thing only was clear though -- they did not wish to be seen together.

Nell looked over at Jack Suhara, who seemed preoccupied. She wondered what he was thinking. She had got off-track from Jack, and onto Moira and Hernandez.

The elevator lurched to its gut-wrenching stop and they disembarked. The tram was nowhere in sight.

"We'll walk," said Jack. "We'll be checking these pipes," and he pointed upwards to two rows of heavy plastic pipe, one black, the other white. The pipes, about four inches in diameter, ran along the tunnel wall about eight feet above the foot path.

"Why are there two lines?" she inquired.

"When we do the filling," he replied, "we have to keep the levels in the acrylic tank and in the rock cavity exactly the same. Otherwise there will be too much strain on the ropes which hold the tank in place. The white pipe will carry the heavy water to the tank, and the black pipe will take the ultrapure water to the cavity."

Now they had caught up with the work crew. There were men up ahead with headlamps and drills, fitting metal brackets into the rock walls. Others were threading the pipe through the brackets and joining the ends with glue and hose clamps.

A broad-shouldered figure with a wide boyish smile approached them.

"Hi, Mr. Suhara. Things are going good, but it's slow drilling the norite."

"Hello Chuck," Jack replied, introducing Nell to the foreman. "I'll be here for a while, checking the elbows and brackets. Would you take Mrs. Fitzgerald down to see how they're doing with the panels?"

"Sure thing," brightened Farraday with a pleased glance at the red-head, and together they mounted the tram and swept down to the base of the cavity, through the double doors, and once again Nell found herself in the great surrealist cavern, intent shadowy figures silhouetted in a distant dream-world, the setting reminiscent of Paradise Lost.

It had been two days since Nell had entered the pit, and work on the lower halves of both tank and dome had progressed dramatically.

"You'd better stay here," said Chuck. "The air's not very good over there -- they're wearing those masks because of the glue."

There was the faint, nauseating smell of acetone, and she was happy to comply. She noticed a fan in the distance and a ventilation pipe she hadn't seen before.

After a few moments Farraday returned, satisfied with the morning's work.

"Are you under time pressure on this project?" asked Nell.

"You *bet* we are! There's political pressure. They got these projects going on all over. Bridges, now he's real impatient to get this thing finished. Suhara, he's more laid back. But it goes as it goes -- when ya rush you make mistakes."

As so often before, Nell appreciated the solid practicality of the people on the front line. "It's where the rubber hits the road," as the workers would say, and the further up the ladder you go the more things get clouded by abstraction and ambition.

Chuck wheeled the tram around and headed back up the hill to the pipe crew. Jack stood frowning, holding a bent bracket in his hand.

"These are too light!" he exclaimed angrily. "I put some weight on it and *look at it!*"

"Probably went to the lowest bidder," put in Chuck dryly.

"That water will be moving fast by the time it hits this level," said Suhara. "These brackets must be changed. Get all the men drilling while we order replacements. If they finish, send them home."

On the way up in the elevator, Jack was visibly upset. "Mike will be angry. How could this happen? We did not have these problems at Kuchino -- in Japan there is *order!*"

Back in the office, Nell found the purchase order for the pipe brackets. Somehow aluminum had been substituted for the stainless steel the design had called for. When Mike came out of the meeting at noon, Jack showed him the purchase order and he hit the roof. He grabbed the phone, punched in the number for the Purchasing Commission in Ottawa, and roared for the name on the purchase order. A sweet voice informed him apologetically that the young officer who had authorized the substitution had gone to lunch.

Bridges hung up, then slammed his fist on the desk. "Christ almighty!" he bellowed. "How in the name of sweet Jesus can I get this bloody thing running with these gimble-nut jackasses in Ottawa fucking around with it! Whose side are they bloody-well *on?* Are they working for the goddamn *competition?"*

Nell decided this would be a good time to set up the tape recorder in the conference room for Dr. Hernandez. As she was removing the equipment from a cupboard, Bridges shouted, "Get me the imbecile who runs that outfit at 1:00!"

"Yessir!" and she hurried out.

By the time she'd set up the equipment it was 12:15. She just had time to drive home, grab a sandwich, and pack a suitcase for her move to the site. As she drove out the project gate, the cell phone rang in her purse. She scrambled for it in time to beat the call-forward.

"It's Siegel. Where are you?"

"In the car, heading home for lunch."

"Good. Moira Houston is the president of a computer games company called AstroLearn. The only product the company makes is an educational game for kids, called StarCourse. It has seven progressive parts. The kids try to work out the future of the universe, from the Big Bang onwards. It's so popular the computer stores are throwing it in as free software on the new machines."

"The game Hernandez was talking about."

"Yes. But listen. The genius who invented the game is Moira's son, Evan. He's a child prodigy. He's only 16, and since his father committed suicide he's been a recluse -- spends all his time on this StarCourse. He's just completing the updated version now."

"Right," said Nell, piecing it together, while another part of

74

her mind dealt with the traffic. "And in the new version there will be no neutrinos...*because Hernandez has got to the kid somehow!* And Moira wants Evan to delay marketing it."

"Precisely," said Siegel.

"I'll be hearing Hernandez in about an hour," said Nell, "and taping him. Mike's orders."

"Good. Make sure you tape the questions as well -- everything that's said. How is everything else?"

"There was nothing unusual I could detect about Jack -- if anything he seems dedicated to the project. We had tea together and then went below. He sent me off to the base with Farraday while he inspected the piping. When we got back, Mr. Suhara had found that they'd been delivered the wrong brackets..."

"Not *another* delay!"

"Mike was in a purple rage when I left. The head of the Purchasing Commission's going to get an earful at 1:00 -- I'm sure you'll be hearing about it."

"How am I going to explain this one to the Minister?" groaned Siegel. "That Commission is staffed by traitors to the country..."

"That's what Mike said," laughed Nell, pulling up in front of the brownstone. "By the way, how did you find out about Evan?"

"On the Internet. I knew Moira was involved in a software company. I found the company under her name on one of the big search engines. I called the company office and raved on and on about StarCourse, how it helped my son get through his physics. The girl couldn't let me speak to Evan Houston, she said, he wasn't well enough, but he'd been a lot better since he'd struck up an e-mail friendship with an old Mexican physicist..."

"...who Moira can't afford to be seen with in public," put in Nell.

"Don't be too hasty," cautioned Siegel. "She has her reputation to consider. Why would she want to be seen with a crank like Hernandez?"

CHAPTER 10

The old man stood at the blackboard, chalk in hand, eyes bright with intent. Around the conference table, seated in a semicircle facing him, the engineers and physicists waited.

The old man introduced himself. "As most of you will remember from my visit in August, I am Dr. Juan Hernandez. I have spent most of my life in fascination over astrophysics." He chuckled. "And as you can see, I have reached the age where I no longer buy green bananas."

At least he has a sense of humour, thought Nell.

"I am here to present to you the fundamental weakness in Einstein's special theory of relativity, and then to offer for your consideration an alternative principle from which to explain the universe."

Nell had strategically positioned herself at five o'clock in the semicircle in order to observe the reactions to this outspoken eccentric, who was finally being allowed his moment in the sun.

"I will get straight to the point. As you know, the neutrino was invented in the early 1930's, when I was a young man, to explain a small amount of missing energy when the nucleus of an atom breaks down into a proton and an electron. Physicists at that time, including Neils Bohr, were faced with the choice of either abandoning the law of conservation of energy, or accepting this hypothetical -- and revolutionary -- neutral particle. The neutrino, though unobserved, was necessary to uphold their basic understanding of the atom.

"In 1938, Hans Bethe developed the first model to explain how energy is produced in the sun, by hydrogen fusion. This model also required the existence of a little neutral particle.

"In 1956, at the Savannah River nuclear reactor in Georgia, a few rare particle interactions were seen over many weeks in a detector the size of a small room. It was concluded that these interactions were being caused by the neutrinos, which were held by atomic theory to be streaming from the reactor.

"Since that time, to confirm both the sun theory *and* the structure of the atom, governments have been spending countless millions to build better and better neutrino detectors. But all attempts to count solar neutrinos have resulted in only one-third to one-half the number required to support the theory of how our sun burns -- the theory of hydrogen fusion.

"To explain this pivotal and upsetting problem, they contrived more imaginary properties for the solar neutrino. They said that solar neutrinos -- which they call electron neutrinos because they activate electrons in the detectors -- were changing mass within the sun and turning into two other kinds of neutrinos which they cannot detect coming from the sun because these neutrinos do not have enough energy to activate the electrons.

"But this idea of changing mass leads into another disturbing contradiction. They say the neutrino travels at the speed of light, like the photon. But the photon travels at the speed of light precisely *because* it has no mass, so how can the neutrino have mass? Now they are in a corner. To get around it, they say that the neutrino has a mass at rest but not while travelling at the speed of light.

"Is this a rational or a compelling theory?

"Ladies and gentlemen, if you still believe in the neutrino, you are clinging to a dream, a superstition, an invention that is unsupported by observation. When you open your Sudbury detector you will count random particle interactions as everyone before you has done. But they will not be neutrinos, because there *are* no neutrinos. You are working with an obsolete model of particle physics, and it has been obsolete since it was conceived, back in my youth."

Nell glanced around. Cam MacAllister wore an expression of pathos, and was sadly shaking his head, as if watching some brilliant mind that had gone off the rails. A quick angry shadow flickered over the face of Miles Oliver, like a tiny cloud over the sun. Hoffman and Mintzman both had their hands up, waiting to speak. Moira was pale with strain, her eyes downcast. Sidney Hawthorpe's fine tremulous hands were folding and unfolding in agitation. Bridges was impatiently tapping his foot. Sam Carney seemed amused and Morgan Washington shrugged his shoulders philosophically, then looked over at the porcelain woman, who was staring at Hernandez in wide, blue-eyed disbelief. Kelly Rowe was watching the old man with sympathetic awe. Robin Kettering was focused intently on some internal thought. Jack Suhara was absent.

Absent! But the only one absent, she realized. He wouldn't try anything now, surely!

Hernandez nodded towards Carl Hoffman to take his question.

"Dr. Hernandez, test after test after test has demonstrated the existence of neutrinos. We isolate them in our accelerators. We accurately predicted the number from the 1987 supernova. And when the Canadian Neutrino Project opens next week, we will finally be able to count the missing tau and muon neutrinos. It is you, sir, who are disregarding the observations."

The old man wore the patient air of one talking to a small child. "Once you have accepted a theoretical framework, and accorded to its inventor the label of genius of the century, and presented Nobel prizes to researchers who claim to have confirmed that theory, you no longer wish to question the framework. It becomes invisible, you live within it as you breathe the air. You see only the evidence you want to see, the evidence that 'fits' the original framework. But throughout history man has replaced the paradigms he has used to understand the universe, and so, too, special relativity will be replaced."

Mintzman had put his hand up again and the old man acknowledged him.

"The particle physics theory and the standard solar model continue to be supported by all the evidence we see, *except* the solar neutrino count. We *do readily* accept inconsistencies and get onto their cases until they are reconciled..."

All heads turned as the crystal voice of Miles Oliver cut across Mintzman's words with finality. "My fellow physicists...here, there is no resolution possible. This man stands outside the solid, time-wrought edifice of modern physics. He is wasting our time. Let him publish as he pleases, let him talk to the journalists. The world will recognize him for what he is -- an egocentric crackpot who never made it to the inside."

There was a moment of stunned silence. Certainly there was agreement that Miles Oliver was right, but Hernandez had been cut off at the knees like a Dickensian schoolboy.

People were preparing to leave. Kelly Rowe stood up and addressed the old man in a kindly tone. "Dr. Hernandez, you mentioned a new paradigm -- if you have time to go into it, I'm sure that some of us would be most interested."

Hernandez flashed a smile of pleasure, picked up the chalk, and turned to the blackboard. Speaking enthusiastically and scribbling like fury, he soon had the board filled with equations, but only Hoffman, Mintzman, Kelly, Robin and Nell had remained in the room.

It was far beyond Nell to judge whether Dr. Hernandez was right or wrong in pointing to a new age for physics; certainly, as Miles Oliver had said, he stood outside the current one. When Dr. Hernandez had finished his presentation he thanked his small audience and asked if there was a phone available to call a taxi. Nell, thinking to learn more of his liaison with Moira, offered to drive him to the airport. Robin, who was standing by waiting to have a word with the old man, asked if he could accompany them. En route to the airport, Nell drove in silence as the two men discoursed animatedly in a language that was foreign to her; the young man light, open, respectful; the elder, a lifetime crusader against a sea of opposition, often rough and impatient.

As they turned off to the airport Nell decided to give it a try.

"Excuse me, Dr. Hernandez," she interrupted. "I don't understand how we can predict neutrinos correctly from a distant supernova, but not from our own sun. How can that be?"

"It cannot be," he said simply. "If the neutrino were a real particle, our observations of it would be consistent. It is true our detectors registered a flux of 19 so-called neutrinos when the 1987 supernova exploded. That star was *one hundred billion* times further away than our sun, which is so close that we bask in its heat and gear our lives to its light. The supernova sends us the 'correct' number of neutrinos to count, but the sun does not. Why not? Because the neutrino is a fantasy."

They were now pulling up in front of the airport, and Hernandez reached for his suitcase and opened the door. As Robin accompanied him into the airport, Nell wondered to herself why a man gnarled with age would spend his twilight years probing the laws of the universe, when the evolving paradigms of human understanding were so transient to him. Robin reappeared and slid nimbly into the car. "You may have just seen history in the making," he said excitedly, latching his seat belt.

"What do you mean?" asked Nell incredulously.

"Wait a bit. We may be in for some action. I'll explain it all later when there's more time."

By the time Nell and Robin swung through the gates in the project's chainlink fence, it was nearly 5:00 and growing dark. When Nell walked into her office, Mike Bridges was preparing to leave for home to shower and change for the dinner in town. Surprisingly, he asked if she would accompany him. She hesitated, decided there was no harm in it, and said yes, she would return on the bus with the others.

Jack appeared briefly to say that because he'd been covering for Mike that day he'd got behind and was going to catch up by working that evening. He was sorry to miss the party. Mike seemed indifferent. Nell, alarmed, realized it was too late to change course and stay on the project as lookout in case Morgan Washington was right about Jack.

She stopped at her trailer to freshen up, and as she hurried through the dark to the parking lot where Mike was warming up his truck, the physicists, who had been in a late afternoon session, came drifting out of the administration building and over to their trailers to dress for the evening.

Meanwhile, unremarkable and unseen in the festive environment, a dark-clad figure slipped into the warehouse, circled around behind the elevator, opened a door marked "Utilities", entered, and pulled a switch.

Nell climbed into the old Bronco. "Jack works awfully hard, doesn't he?" she asked, testing. "And so does Moira Houston. I didn't see her come out with the others just now."

"Jack's got the Jap work ethic, all right. Moira wasn't feeling so hot this afternoon and went off to her room with a headache."

"Oh, that's too bad!" exclaimed Nell, wondering how in heaven's name she could be going off and leaving the project open to the devices of Jack and Moira. God hope that night watchman is on his toes tonight, she thought. "Last night she seemed so perky," she added.

"She's been in bad shape ever since her husband died," answered Bridges. "He was diagnosed with Lou Gehrig's disease, but that's not what killed him. He did himself in a couple of years ago. It wasn't pretty -- blew his brains all over the kitchen ceiling. It drove their son 'round the bend and Moira's all bound up with guilt."

"It wasn't her fault he made that choice -- but if she was away from home a lot with her work, she probably feels responsible."

"Dunno," he said. "She's all over the place."

"She seemed pretty friendly towards you," Nell teased, casting a coy smile across the darkened cab.

"Probably lonely, he answered vaguely, and turned on the radio, signalling end of discussion.

Nell waited while Bridges showered. He appeared briefly in the hallway in boxer shorts, toweling his hair, the scent of after-shave drifting towards her. The physical reality of the man, his solid shoulders and matted chest summoned in her a curious and unexpected wave of desire. She briefly imagined her own bareness against the barrel chest and the hardness of him. Desire escalated painfully. A purely sexual act, she thought, not an intimacy. And married. And the brusque project boss. Forget it, she told herself firmly, and opened the rolled-up newspaper. She fixed upon a brief mention that the Canadian Neutrino Project, which had been subject to delays, was due to open November 17th, with a ribbon-cutting ceremony to be presided over by the Minister of Industry Canada. Several dozen top-ranking world physicists would be in attendance. The press release had been issued from Ottawa.

"You ready?" he asked, standing in the hall with his hand on the door. She quickly refolded the newspaper and passed in front of him, his arm circling nearly around her as he reached to turn off the lights. Again the pang of desire; she gave no sign of it by word or glance. Biz had bet Mike was straight in his marriage and Nell resolved to betray no hint of her newfound vulnerability to the man.

At six o'clock Nell and Bridges pulled up at the Civic Square on Larch Street, just as the driver wheeled the CNP charter bus around the corner, sliding it to a smooth halt in front of the Peter Piper Inn. The party spilled out of the bus in high spirits and divided up into groups. Mike, Biz, Miles Oliver, the porcelain woman, Carl Hoffman, Harry Mintzman, and Morgan Washington headed off in search of a steakhouse, choosing their steps carefully along the ice-rutted sidewalk. Nell, Alex Wong, Kelly Rowe, Cam MacAllister, Sam Carney, and Robin Kettering set out in the opposite direction for pasta before catching the 8:00 symphony at the theatre. The others would attend the movies of their choice.

Nell was seated between Kelly and Alex. The men spoke of old Hernandez with a kind of grudging admiration, though it was clear they rejected his views. Nell remembered the porcelain woman and asked Kelly who she was. Kelly was certainly on top of things -- Dr. Hilaire Modeste was on loan from CERN in Geneva, where she had worked for some years as the assistant to the accelerator's head of research. Single herself, rumour had it that she had been secretly in love with this brilliant man, though unfortunately for Hilaire he was married. She had thrown her heart and soul into the work but in the end the situation had become too much for her -- she had pulled up stakes and come to Canada to join the international project. She had no trouble getting on; while working in Geneva she had become a respected physicist in her own right.

Apart from this it had been an evening of light social interaction that did not afford any clues to the vulnerability of the project.

As arranged, the bus was waiting at 10:45 under a street lamp, puffing exhaust into the frosty air. Mike bid them all good night as they climbed aboard, Nell in a mood of solid contentment after the strains of Beethoven's E-major string quartet and the lyricism of Schubert's ninth symphony. They arrived back at the project just after eleven, with old Harry tipping his cap and reporting that all had been quiet on the site.

◆

When Nell entered the cafeteria at eight o'clock on Friday morning the room was crammed with the work crews from the underground observatory andthere was an excited buzz in the air. Waiting to pay for her breakfast she could hear snatches of conversation. "God, were we ever lucky! It could have blown sky high!" "Someone's going to have to answer for this!" "Thank heaven for Farraday's quick thinking!"

She looked around and spotted Cam MacAllister talking to Sam Carney at a far table.

"May I join you for a moment?" she asked. "What on earth has happened?"

"Sure, sit down!" said MacAllister. "These folks have all had a close call. When they got down to the pit this morning around seven, the place was reeking with acetone. Anything could have set it off -- a blowtorch, a match, even a spark would have caused a large explosion, probably enough to collapse the cavity."

"Was anyone hurt?" she asked, inwardly cursing her night on the town.

"Fortunately not. That Farraday took things in hand. He ordered everyone up to the showers and sealed off the pit and the control room. He called up top to get them to start the emergency air return fan. The crews below had to walk back along the tunnel and get up topside.

"What was wrong with the fan?" asked Nell, fearing the worst.

"We don't know yet. Breakdowns happen -- there's a lot of old equipment around here."

Sam Carney was watching Cam with an air of puzzlement bordering on relief. Nell excused herself and headed for the office. As she walked along the hall the penny dropped. Sam Carney had just realized that there was sabotage involved, and that his son was innocent of the elevator incident last August.

She could hear Mike's urgent voice on the telephone and entered her own office from the hallway.

"...beyond a joke when we're putting lives at stake! We've got a madman here, make no mistake!"

Then a pause while he listened. She popped her head into the doorway to alert him to her presence. He waved her off impatiently.

"All right, all right! But if I can't bring in the police I'm going to document my recommendation..."

Another pause, then he rang off.

"God *damn* that Siegel, what's the bloody *matter* with him? What's so precious about all these pet geniuses of his? Somebody is out to wreck this place and we should close it down 'til there's been a proper investigation!"

"Where's Jack?" asked Nell.

"He worked late, he'll be in around coffee," he answered, waving off the question. "The call from Farraday came straight to me. I went right over to the utility room myself and Jesus Christ if the fan switch wasn't turned *off!* We *tape* the bugger *on* so there can be no mistake...somebody pulled the bloody tape off so this was no accident!"

"Cam says it could blown have up," said Nell.

"Damn rights! Big shock wave -- the rock's under stress, it could bloody-well fracture and the whole thing cave in!"

"Could someone have been playing a prank or something?" she asked, in disbelief.

"Not a hope. There's a sign right under the switch: 'Danger! Never turn off.' There's a sign on the door, too: 'Authorized Personnel Only'."

"Whoever pulled that switch is risking lives..."

"Tell me about it! We're doubling up on security, round the clock. And no one's to go down alone. Siegel's got some kind of plan up his sleeve. He wants to talk to Robin Kettering."

Nell paused to think. What had Robin said? There was going to be some action...history was in the making...he needed more time to explain...

"I'll find him and tell him if you like."

"Do that. And keep quiet about that switch. I'll get a guard stationed over there in the warehouse -- a *plainclothesman* he says! The crew can go back down as soon as Farraday gives the all-clear," and he snatched up the telephone to carry out Siegel's order.

As Nell put on her coat to search for Robin, she was struck by an icicle of foreboding. This neutrino hunt was a high-stakes game. It was now obvious that the force behind this subversion would stop at nothing, and the establishment was protecting its own.

She was just out the door when Robin rounded the corner from the cafeteria, lips pursed in consternation, eyes grave.

"Siegel wants to speak with you," she said urgently. "Mike's just been talking to him."

"Phone upstairs?" he asked briefly. She nodded. He took them two at a time.

CHAPTER 11

An air of oppression hung over the office that morning. The project had taken on an unreal quality and Nell was debating whether she would remain on the site for the weekend or not. The real world beckoned from beyond. Perhaps she would fly to Toronto to visit Betty Sable, the woman she had met on the flight. The thought cheered her considerably.

She picked up the project schedule which Mike had given her after seeing her dismay over the imminent ribbon-cutting. Indeed, the project was nearing its completion. Yesterday, Thursday, the two enormous halves of the great acrylic tank had been fitted together on the platform at the base of the pit and bonded. That bonding must have caused the fumes. She knocked on Mike's door to ask who had been privy to the schedule and was told that it had been circulated in the general business meeting. Everyone knew except her, it seemed.

Today, Friday, the final panels of photomultiplier tubes would be added to the geodesic dome, and its halves too would be joined and bolted. Mike's call to the Purchasing Commission had evidently produced results, for the brackets had arrived late Thursday and the pipes would be in place in time for the water system tests on Saturday morning. The bulkhead doors between the tunnel and the floor of the pit would then be hydraulically shut and the filling of the acrylic tank and its surrounding cavity would begin. A parade of tankers bearing the heavy water and the ultrapure would deliver their cargoes around the clock from Saturday afternoon until late Wednesday morning. Meanwhile, on Monday and Tuesday, Kelly, Alex, and Biz would hook up the computers in the control room to the mass of fine wiring which would carry the neutrino signals from the photomultipliers.

So much for the technical stuff. What would the physicists be doing? She turned to their timetable. Today they would attend a workshop reviewing papers on dark matter. This afternoon at three, a group of physics students from Laurentian University would arrive at the site to hear a lecture by Miles Oliver. They would then be taken down to the observatory to see the completed assembly from the base, before the filling of the cavity on Saturday. The engineers, including Jack Suhara and Sam Carney, would be down there most of the day, checking the final stages of the outer dome, and supervising the pipe connections to the tank and pit.

Tomorrow, Saturday, would be a free day for the physicists. Nell had arranged car rentals for some of them to go shopping and cross-country skiing. Hawthorpe had already rented a car at the airport. In the afternoon a graduate student, Zack Meyer from McGill University, would be on hand to demonstrate websites on the Internet. Mike, Jack, Carney, Washington, and Farraday would be testing the system for leaks all morning. Later in the day they would begin monitoring the heavy and the ultrapure as they gurgled their way deep into the Precambrian Shield.

On Sunday morning Siddhu was to give another talk on physics and consciousness. Nell realized she had not seen him since Wednesday night, then remembered Robin saying he had gone off to a lake cabin to relax and meditate. On Sunday afternoon the project scientists and engineers would be taken on a tour of the completed underground facility. Monday morning the physicists were to hold a panel discussion at Laurentian University on the significance of the neutrino. In the afternoon there would be a second Internet session at the project site, covering newsgroups and listservs. Tuesday was wrap-up, then planning the agendas for coming workshops, and finally, the ribbon-cutting on Wednesday.

Still a long way to go, she thought, with some unknown evil intention lying in wait. A sense of the sinister passed through her, lifting the hair on the nape of her neck.

She was faced with forces she scarcely understood. From

Ottawa, the unrelenting demand that the project finish on schedule. Dr. Washington had said that neutrino observatories were springing up everywhere, in this race to remove this stubborn neutrino from the ointment of astrophysics. Had the facility been infiltrated by someone from another project? Was there a fox among the chickens?

Or was it a darker force born of prestige and power that sought to stall -- or prevent altogether -- the demise of the standard model?

Everyone agreed that the Sudbury facility would have the sensitivity to produce definitive results, to settle the matter once and for all. There would be winners and losers in this game of formulas and theories -- a game, suddenly, of life and death -- and Nell had landed squarely in the middle of it. Even Siegel seemed to be pulling strings, and now Robin was involved. Yes, it would be lovely to air it all to Betty Sable, or call Galiano and spill it to Sonia. But she thought better of it -- relieving the pressure would simply take the edge off her keenness to delve and to comprehend, which was the job she had come to do.

She decided to go early for coffee, take some paperwork, and sit in the corner of the cafeteria by the windows. When the physics group came in for coffee she would listen, under the guise of work.

Just then Robin looked into the office and motioned her out to the corridor.

"You've probably guessed," he said in a low voice. "I'm part of this thing too -- working with Siegel, like you. It's starting to look dangerous. Watch yourself -- be extremely careful. If you run into a problem, you can count on me..."

"What kind of a problem?" she asked, wide-eyed.

"We're dealing with a fanatic. If you discover who it is, you'll be in danger. You can trust me, and you can trust Mike. Beyond that I'm not sure."

"Mike is stepping up security."

"Yes. Siegel asked him to bring in a pipefitter while they're filling the tanks. He'll sleep on a cot in the warehouse. It's plausible enough -- if a join breaks they'll need him on the double."

"Can he actually fix pipes?"

88

"Good question -- probably not!"

"I'll be sitting in the cafeteria when they break for coffee, hard at work in a corner. I want to listen."

"Good. I'll join the group a few minutes after they come in. See if you can hear what is said as I enter the cafeteria."

"Really? Okay."

"We shouldn't be seen together," said Robin. "If anything happens, I'm in trailer D, Room 7."

"D-7," repeated Nell. I was just in a bit of a funk there, after the switch thing. I'm glad you stopped by."

"See you later," he smiled reassuringly. "Got to get back to the workshop!"

As Nell was leaving the office a husky young man in blue coveralls and red-checked shirt came ambling in. He smiled in a carefree sort of way and asked for Mike.

"Are you the pipefitter?" asked Nell.

"That's me!" he beamed. "I'm Ron."

She took him in to meet Bridges, then set off for the cafeteria.

Nell guessed that the morning's agenda would not have permitted general discussion of the near explosion. She was right. Hoffman and Mintzman came in with Cam, got coffee, and took seats by the window, not far away. They were involved in a technical discussion about MSW, which was Greek to her.

Hoffman pulled out his pipe and was loading it when Cam remarked that the underground crews had left the cafeteria and must be back at work. Hoffman and Mintzman seemed scantly interested in the event, good thing no one was hurt, they said, and returned to the MSW discussion. Evidently the "old equipment" story was what was circulating; there was certainly no suggestion of sabotage. Sidney Hawthorpe and Miles Oliver came next, picked up their tea, and joined the threesome.

"MSW is it today?" asked Hawthorpe, in good spirits. "Shouldn't it be G.U.T?"

The others chuckled. Nothing had changed. It seemed that the perpetrator of this morning's failed disaster could believe that he or she had escaped suspicion. Smart of Siegel to play it low key and quietly step up security.

Next, immersed in a discussion about Cerenkov light, Kelly and Moira took a table further away. When Alex and Biz arrived,

Kelly waved them over to join the discussion. The mood at the table changed abruptly as Alex related the morning mishap. Evidently Kelly and Moira had gone straight to the workshop that morning without visiting the cafeteria.

Mike and Washington appeared next, walking through the cafeteria in silence and out into the parking lot. Through the window, Nell could see Washington's earnest face and urgent gestures. Mike laid a hand on his shoulder, said something, and Washington relaxed. The two men came back inside, stomping the snow off their boots, and joined Sam Carney and Jack Suhara, who had just taken seats. She could hear Sam Carney's California voice: the last of the photomultiplier panels were now in the pit, assembly was going smoothly.

Hilaire Modeste arrived and joined the women, followed by Robin, who stood alone at the counter, considering the pies.

"Enter twinkle-toes," said Hawthorpe.

"Ah yes," sighed Miles. "Are we ready for Godphysics this morning?"

"Too esoteric for me!" said Mintzman.

Evidently Robin returned their sentiments, for he joined the ladies.

"Interesting paper on dark matter," commented Hoffman, examining his pipe and relighting it. "I'm really inclined to agree that when we get the missing neutrinos, we'll have dark matter solved as well."

"I admire your confidence, old boy," Miles remarked casually.

"Carl's probably right," said Hawthorpe. "If we get the numbers we want, there'll be enough neutrinos out there to account for the missing dark matter we need for the Big Bang."

"And the Big Crunch," added Mintzman. "Good thing we won't be here to see it!"

"The next few weeks will be very interesting," said Hoffman. "We'll know soon what the trend will be."

Miles Oliver excused himself and went for a refill. Returning, he eyed Nell and veered over to her table.

"May I interrupt?" he asked pleasantly.

"Not at all!" she declared, flattered by his approach.

"We were just discussing the Big Bang," he explained. "I've taught it so many times I thought it more fun to talk to a young lady..."

"...but not about the Big Bang?" she laughed. "I suppose I should know what it is, but..."

"You don't know what it is? You *can't* be serious! Well, listening to them on the subject and telling you about it are two different things! Would you care for an explanation?"

"Oh yes, I'd love one!" she gushed, aware of her pleasure at the prospect of a second lesson from this engaging celebrity.

"We believe," he began, in his comfortable and dignified way, "that the universe began with an enormous, intensely hot explosion. From that single, central outburst there radiated billions upon billions of quarks, the tiniest, most indivisible building blocks of our intricately structured universe..."

Nell became aware that conversation had stopped at the next table. She glanced over to see Cam MacAllister sitting back in his chair, head cocked to one side to better hear the splendid erudition of his English colleague behind him. The heads of Mintzman and Hoffman too were bent in appreciative silence as this simple and elegant history unfolded.

"From this vast initial spray of quarks, partnerships formed in varying patterns to produce the next layer of matter, the protons and neutrons, which bound together in a nucleus to form the atoms.

"The first atom to form -- hydrogen, which is the lightest and most abundant substance in the universe -- contained only one proton and one neutron in its nucleus. Great clouds of hydrogen swirled about, clouds so immense that as they cooled gravity compressed their enormous masses into dense hot cores. The heat at these cores drove the hydrogen nuclei into furious action -- they bounced together like popping corn, their protons fusing into helium, discharging as they did so cascades of heat and light. The clouds literally caught fire to become the stars and the sun..."

Miles Oliver was sitting casually erect, lost in the origins of the universe, when the scraping of chairs and a tap on the shoulder by Cam MacAllister returned him to the present moment.

"Young lady, it seems I must repair to the conference room. Do come to my lecture this afternoon! You will hear all of this and more."

"Why thanks, Dr. Oliver!" replied Nell warmly. "I believe I

will."

There was a general exodus from the cafeteria, while Robin hung back to catch Nell's eye. He held up his watch and tapped at twelve on the dial, eyebrows raised in question. She nodded and pointed to her office.

At 10:30 Mike Bridges, Jack Suhara, Sam Carney, and Morgan Washington rode the lift down together, bearing trays of steaming coffee and Danish pastries for the work crews.

Sam Carney was in a thoughtful mood, and suddenly said to Mike, "How come that return-air ventilator broke down? Aren't there backup safety standards in place here in Canada?"

Washington murmured agreement to the question.

Mike and Jack Suhara looked at each other. Mike quickly weighed his answer, then replied.

"You're right, you're ahead of us with safety standards -- you folks lead the way. Canada is a poorer country, fewer people."

"You mean there's no backup to the system?" pursued Carney in astonishment.

"There are some big electric fans down there, but nothing that kicks in automatically," said Mike carefully.

"Are those fans working now?" asked Washington.

Jack Suhara spoke. "The main system is working again."

"How did you fix it so fast?" asked Carney, with growing suspicion.

"It wasn't broken," conceded Mike. "Someone flicked the switch."

"Christ!" breathed Carney. "That's no accident!"

"We don't know yet," said Mike, sliding away from the truth. "We're investigating. There are undercover people here keeping a close eye on things."

Carney frowned, processing the implications.

"It could be anybody," he said. "Your only other alternative is to close the whole thing down -- send everybody home and hire new crews."

"That's about it," agreed Mike flatly. "And we all know we're not going to do that. So let's keep it to ourselves, shall we?"

The cage lurched to it's usual halt, and Mike met each man's eye in turn, testing for consent. They all nodded, the doors opened, and they crossed the apron to the tram.

At twelve noon Robin Kettering quietly opened the hall door into Nell's office and looked inquiringly towards Bridges' office. Nell nodded and whispered, "I'll meet you in the little room upstairs, next to the dining lounge."

Robin departed promptly and Nell picked up her purse containing the cell phone, then quickly mounted the linoleum stairs and entered the little office.

"We need to talk," whispered Robin urgently. "I'm going to go for a run at lunchtime...could you get away and join me?"

"Jack will be back up just before one," thought Nell out loud. "I could run between one and two."

"Good! I'll give you a head start. Say you start about 1:10...I'll leave a little after quarter past and catch you up. Probably best to run towards town -- the roads are ploughed that way."

"See you out there," she replied, withdrawing.

She returned via the cafeteria, picking up a sandwich and a cup of tea. The time passed slowly. At ten to one she heard Jack Suhara enter Mike's office and give a report on the work below. The final assembly was running like clockwork and the crews were making up for lost time.

Mike asked Jack if he had seen the pipefitter on his way through the warehouse; he had not. Probably gone for lunch, muttered Mike. Mike's face appeared in Nell's doorway.

"When are you going for lunch?" he asked.

"About one," she replied. "I need some fresh air -- I'm going for a run."

"Just check the warehouse and make sure that pipefitter's around."

Nell gathered up her purse and coat, crossed the compound, and heaving on the heavy door, entered the dimly lit old building. Her eyes adjusted to the light -- there was no sign of the pipefitter. She was just about to walk around behind the elevator when the doors opened and Sidney Hawthorpe stepped out, alone and shaken. He shifted defensively, then explained rather awkwardly that he'd been down to have a look before they filled it. As Siegel had ordered that no one go down alone, she asked if he had cleared it with Mike.

"Oh, don't worry about him!" he replied quickly. "I've been down many times before -- Mike knows that."

Hawthorpe then bowed away and hurried off toward the parking lot.

Upon reflection Nell realized that Hawthorpe would have been seen by the engineers and the work crews below, and that opportunities to do damage, should he have wished to, would have been extremely limited. She was getting paranoid. Suddenly she couldn't wait to cleanse her mind and body with a long invigorating run.

CHAPTER 12

Nell let herself into the cold trailer room and rummaged through her suitcase for the faded blue and green sweat-suit she had worn so often. She laced up the new Adidas, ran a brush through her hair, and did a few warm-up stretches.

She pocketed her room key and trotted out across the compound to the parking lot. The pipefitter was just coming out of the cafeteria; he smiled and raised a mock salute before turning back towards the warehouse. Nell ran out between the chain-link gates, then down the company road for half a mile to the stop sign at the main road. She turned left towards town, and with the snow firm beneath her feet, opened up her stride.

The day was clear and cold. There was not a breath of wind. Nell ran along the silent road through the clean, snowbright landscape, her cheeks tingling and her breath visible on the frosty air. The flat rolling hills opened up under the great dome of northern sky. She entered a stretch of light woodland; still trees with cracked white birch-bark stood out in the pale reflected light. A red squirrel scurried across the road ahead, then another. Chickadees darted to and fro in the wintry lace above.

A clear liquid whistle rang out from the left. Nell promptly turned, running on the spot, and craned to locate the source of this crystal purity. She retraced her steps a little, then stopped short in astonishment. Poised in scarlet splendour on a silver branch of birch sat a black-faced crested cardinal, larger than life. She could scarcely believe her eyes, watching in wonderment this magnificent bird with its pink cone-shaped beak, sitting huddled on one foot to keep the other warm.

Nell became aware of movement in her peripheral vision and glanced back down the road to see a man running lightly towards her. Robin! She ran back to meet him, then signalled him to slow down, while she breathlessly explained about the cardinal.

Robin slowed to a walk, and they carefully approached the spot. The cardinal, unperturbed, looked benignly down upon them with warm brown eyes, then shifted its vivid red plumage to the other foot.

Robin laughed and said, "Richmondena cardinalis himself. What a treat!"

The bird, as if to entertain them, spread its wings and dropped silently into the snow, sprawling its glistening crimson wings about in the fluffy whiteness, as if to bathe. Nell was enchanted; she put a hand to Robin's arm and smiled up at him like a happy child. He, too, was touched by the moment, his own expression sliding over the top of happiness into gravity. Nell recognized in him an aspect of herself, an overflow of feeling which could collapse toward tears.

Abruptly the bird, having performed its magic upon them, spread its wings and arced ahead of them through the trees to alight on the snowy branch of an old spruce. There it raised a wing and began comfortably to preen.

Without a word, Robin and Nell resumed their run, and as they passed the now preoccupied cardinal, Nell looked back in reluctant farewell.

They settled into a rhythmic running pattern, the rawboned man in khaki shorts covering the ground with ease. Nell, falling behind, admired his loping elegance. She lengthened and quickened her own stride to keep up. Though the purpose of the run was to discuss the project, neither now wished to break the cardinal's spell, so they ran in silence, occasionally glancing at one another to nod agreement that it was still too early to give up this welcome diversion.

Presently they approached the highway, a much busier route with traffic coming and going. Robin pulled up and looked at his watch. "One thirty-five. We'd better stop now, and walk back."

"Too bad," she murmured, out of breath. "We've run out of road...it's depressing, turning back."

96

"Something very dark is going on," he agreed, "but with luck we should know who's behind it before long."

"Do you really think so? I've been finding it rather hopeless."

"My role is to set a trap for the guilty party," he explained. "Some weeks ago I heard whispers of trouble and I contacted Siegel from Vancouver. Siegel may be a bureaucrat but he sees the big picture. I proposed a plan and he agreed to let me make the necessary arrangements. Now it looks as though we have begun to draw the quarry out."

"What on earth do you mean?" she exclaimed.

"You can look at physics -- including astrophysics -- as a kind of mind game," said Robin. "Most physicists see it as a fascinating quest for knowledge, and they get paid to boot. But, as Siegel may have told you, some take it too seriously. They want security in knowledge, and when they think they've got it, they commit the Buddhist sin of *attachment* to it."

Nell thought of her own attachments. Patrick, the beach house, the flowers, the parrot. "Attachments define us," she said simply.

"Yes and no," he replied. "At one level, yes, they anchor us in our identity and our pleasures. But there is a deeper level in us which is sublime and which does not need these things."

"Like seeing the cardinal."

"Exactly. It was completely gratuitous and in that way more special than anything we could own or plan to experience."

"Unpredictable, unsolicited -- a surprise and a delight," she added. "A gift from the gods."

"Absolutely! A gift. And that is a way of living -- watching what is 'given' to our senses as it unfolds, as a series of gifts, without particularly needing to own things and to tie our satisfactions and energies to them."

"Most people wouldn't trust that, they'd be bored," she said.

"Because they are so strongly defined by what they own, and by adding to it," he answered. "But defining ourselves that way is narcissistic and self-involved. And it stifles our capacity to look out and fully absorb what is given gratuitously."

"Self-involvement kills receptivity to life," she replied.

"Precisely. So there are self-involved physicists, and there are receptive physicists. The receptive ones are fascinated, purely and simply. They follow the evidence wherever it leads. Do you see how Hoffman and Mintzman are so in love with the neutrino question? I bet you they'd never dream of harming the project."

"I've noticed it too," agreed Nell. "They're almost inseparable in their curiosity -- they can hardly wait for the results!"

"Like two children on Christmas Eve," he smiled, then sobered. "But my guess is, there is someone here pathologically attached to a point of view in the neutrino controversy, a point of view which may be proved wrong. It's possible that we can make that someone edgy enough to strike again. And that is why we have had Dr. Hernandez and Siddhu here this week."

Robin paused to let this sink in.

Dr. Hernandez and Siddhu are decoys?"

"In a word, yes. They are both highly unconventional thinkers whose articulate doubts about the current paradigm could stress someone with a vested interest to the breaking point."

"I wonder why Mr. Siegel didn't mention..."

Nell was cut off in mid-sentence by the sound of a car approaching fast from behind. As they turned, a pale blue Sprint shot over the crest of the hill towards them. It's driver, panicked by the sudden appearance of people, braked hard, and the little car spun out of control on the snowy road, angling straight at them. Nell caught a glimpse of Sydney Hawthorpe's grim, bespectacled face behind a frenzy of elbows at the wheel.

An iron grip caught Nell across the lower ribs and in one deft motion she was whisked across the ditch and into a large clump of grass to land face-down in the snow. She raised herself up on an elbow; Robin was in push-up position beside her, head craned around to watch the little car disappearing down the road, tooting wildly.

He sank back into the snow, brown eyes intent, and reached over to smooth the wet hair back from her brow.

"Are you all *right?*" he asked, peering closely into her face.

Nell sat up, then smiled reassuringly. "No broken bones, just a little shaken up," she said. "It happened so fast!"

"I think I over-reacted," he said apologetically.

They got up, brushed themselves off, then Nell glanced at the skid-marks. "You *didn't* over-react! His tracks ran right over our footsteps!"

"Why the hell didn't he stop?" cried Robin. "What godawful driving!"

"Perhaps he's not used to the snow," she suggested.

"He's from Pennsylvania, isn't he? And he rented the car at the airport and drove it here in a snowstorm!"

"What are you saying?" asked Nell in disbelief. "That he would deliberately try to run us down?"

"I don't know," said Robin. "It's just uncanny that he didn't stop to check on us -- especially when he knows us!"

Nell suddenly remembered Hawthorpe's solitary trip down the mine. "That reminds me!" she said. "Mike sent me into the warehouse to look for the pipefitter just before I left on my run, and I saw Dr. Hawthorpe come out of the lift by himself. He was all tensed up and seemed embarrassed to see me."

"So that was only forty-five minutes ago?"

"Yes. He said he just wanted to have a look before they filled it up. Apparently he's been down several times and doesn't bother clearing it with Mike."

"Hmmm...do you remember how he reacted when Siddhu spoke after dinner on Wednesday night?"

"I sure do! He was in a fit of pique, behaving like a spoilt child!"

"Worried about his grand unification theory, no doubt," said Robin.

"Oh yes!" recalled Nell. "You're twinkle-toes."

"What!"

"That's what he said when you came into the restaurant this morning -- 'here comes twinkle-toes.' And Miles Oliver added, 'Anyone for Godphysics?'"

"Now that's hostility," commented Robin dryly. "Not particularly objective, is it?"

Nell was silent for a moment. "Robin there are just *too many* suspicious people around here! Moira's afraid because of her son's computer game. Washington thinks Jack Suhara has a motive. Siegel thinks Washington could just as easily have a motive. And now we've got Hawthorpe acting like a lunatic, and even Dr. Oliver is hostile!"

"Siegel filled me in this morning on what you told him about Moira, and about Washington," said Robin. "You know, there could be two or more people in this thing together..."

"I wonder why Mr. Siegel didn't tell me that you're working with him," she remarked again.

"He didn't want to influence you," said Robin. "He let me set up these meetings to test my hunch, but he wanted you to work alone, freshly, from your own perspective."

"That makes sense, I guess. I'm going to call him and ask him to check on Hawthorpe."

"Good idea. The man's a loose cannon. How the devil's he going to explain himself?"

"Probably avoid us," she answered. "It's pathetic."

"I'd like to confront him," said Robin, "but if he's our man it might throw him off." He looked at his watch. "It's getting late. Are you up to running back?"

"Oh yes, I'd prefer to run."

"You'd better get a head start so we don't arrive together. Talk to you later -- I'll be tied up in the meeting until three."

"OK," said Nell. "I'll be in the office until three, then I'll be going to Dr. Oliver's lecture and after that I'll be helping with the student tour down the mine."

"I'll keep an eye on Hawthorpe. I'll alert the pipefitter not to let him go down again. How will I contact you?"

"Call me anytime on the cellular phone. You can use the little office upstairs," and she broke into a run, heart heavy as she approached the unreal world of the project and the diseased mind plotting destruction within it. The place was beginning to give her the willies.

Back in her trailer, Nell put through a call to Siegel in Ottawa. He was in the office, but had to be paged.

"Mr. Siegel? Nell here. There have been some unpleasant developments."

"I know about the ventilation switch," he put in quickly.

"Good," said Nell. "I've just had a run with Robin. We're now working in sync."

"Yes, I thought that switch incident might bring you together," he replied. "And that's for the good. Things are escalating. You'll both be safer working together."

"The latest is that just before one o'clock I saw Hawthorpe

100

getting out of the elevator alone, looking upset. The pipefitter was at lunch. And while Robin and I were out jogging along the road just now, Hawthorpe burst over the crest of a hill, slammed on his brakes, skidded wildly towards us, forcing us off the road, and didn't even bother to stop. If Robin hadn't thrown me over the ditch I would have been run down."

"He sounds mad!" declared Siegel. "Which way was he going?"

"Coming from town, overtaking us on our way back to the project."

"All right, I'll do some checking...I'll get back to either you or Robin later this afternoon."

"Oh, and his behaviour at Siddhu's dinner talk on Wednesday night was downright peevish," Nell added.

"Was it indeed?" He could be dangerous, if he's our man. Watch yourself, Mrs. O'Donovan, don't go running alone. Siddhu will be giving a second talk Sunday morning -- that might precipitate another attempt."

"I'll be careful," and they rang off.

CHAPTER 13

About a dozen physics students and two faculty members from Laurentian University arrived on the project at 2:45. Bridges was on hand to greet them and take them on a short above-ground tour of the site. Meanwhile, Nell rearranged the dining-hall chairs into lecture-room configuration, and ordered coffee up from the cafeteria.

At 3:00 the students filed in, helped themselves to coffee, and took seats. Biz and Hilaire Modeste turned up, followed by Morgan Washington.

Miles Oliver entered and headed purposefully for the blackboard, where in a brisk hand he wrote, "The Role of the Neutrino in Stellar Evolution," then turned to face the class. After briefly surveying the group he held up a hand and the room fell silent. His manner was powerful, Dickensian.

"I promise you the lecture won't take long," he said cheerfully, "and then you'll have the rare privilege of visiting a state-of-the-art subterranean neutrino laboratory." He raised a hand again to quell a ripple of appreciation from the students, then began.

"As I promised a young lady here in the audience," nodding towards Nell, "we shall begin our account with the primary event you have all no doubt heard described, the Big Bang -- the flashpoint which created our universe. That post-explosion universe was so hot and the collisions between its particles so violent that only the most fundamental, indivisible particles could survive intact. These were the quarks, and as you know, we have recently verified the existence of the top, and final, quark..."

Nell marvelled at the man. Miles Oliver was a portrait of human civility: polished, poised, humourous, erudite. He warmed to his performance, adrift in a sea of melodic lucidity, his casual bearing in easy control, an actor lost in the part. Nell glanced about the room; every face was turned upwards in rapt attention.

"...so that today we accord to this unique particle a powerful role in the unfolding of the universe. It is present by the trillions in every recess, it surges from supernovae billions of light years distant, it streams from the reactor that powers our sun, and it may even account for the mysteriously absent dark matter which we have yet to identify..."

A peripheral movement caught Nell's eye; it was a hand going up, rather tentatively, off to the right. It's owner was a young Indonesian lad, slender as a fawn.

"Excuse me, sir?" asked a polite voice.

Miles Oliver blinked in surprise, as if awakening from a trance. A quick angry frown crossed his face.

"What is it?" he snapped crossly.

The boy was taken aback. "I'm sorry sir. I should not have interrupted."

Miles Oliver remembered himself and beamed encouragement. "No matter, boy. What is your question?"

"Well, sir, it's just that the evidence for the role of the neutrino seems contradictory. How can science be so sure about the neutrino when we can never count more than one-third of the predicted number, and when the fluxes from the 1987 Supernova arrived at different times?"

"Youth," laughed Oliver, "has a healthy curiosity, but is often inclined to take the controversial position. Young man, the subject is much more complex than you indicate. There are different kinds of neutrinos, with different masses. Within a few weeks we shall be able to detect them all, at which time the counts will be corrected."

"Yes, sir. You will be able to count the muon and tau neutrinos as well as the electron neutrinos."

"That is what makes this facility unique," explained Miles, taking the time now. "It is orders of magnitude more sensitive than the earlier detectors. And it will be the lowest background-radiation site on the planet. All right?"

"Except that the 1987 supernova results were inconsistent," the boy persisted.

Miles laughed at the young man's intentness. "Again, my boy, that was a matter of varying equipment sensitivities. There is far too much theoretical and observational evidence to doubt the presence of the neutrino. We need only devise the instrumentation to intercept it." He concluded the interruption on a note of finality, and returned to his flow of thought.

True to his word, Miles Oliver smoothly encapsulated the role of the neutrino in stellar evolution in a delightfully brief and stimulating lecture. He then glanced at his pocket watch and looked at Nell. "Now I understand that it will take some time for us all to get down to the mine and shower and so forth. I suggest that you hold any questions until we get below. I believe that Mrs. Fitzgerald will be escorting us?"

"Yes, I'll be helping Mr. Suhara with the tour," replied Nell. "We've arranged to meet him at the lift at 3:45."

The lecture session broke up.

Morgan Washington turned to Hilaire Modeste. "I spent most of the day down that mine. Would you care to join me for a cup of coffee?"

Hilaire's eyes brightened. "I would love that, yes. I shall be going down on Sunday, and once will be enough!"

The group arrived at the cage to find Jack Suhara awaiting them, courteous but stone-faced. The students piled in and the antiquated lift rumbled and lurched down the interminable shaft. Some of the group fell silent while others made nervous jokes about the journey to the centre of the earth, lift breakdowns, mineshaft collapses, and heroic rescue missions. Nell stood beside Biz and held her focus on the students' chatter to contain her own discomfort.

In time they reached bottom, and Jack Suhara drove Biz, Nell, the two faculty and three girls, while Miles Oliver and the young men hiked along the tunnel at a brisk pace behind the tram. As they approached the observatory they passed Farraday and his crew fitting the final pipe brackets into the black norite. Nell took the girls in for showers and then everyone met in the control room for a lively explanation of the computer functions from Biz.

The group, wearing fresh coveralls, stood around Biz in a semi-circle, facing the computers.

"Below us hangs a huge vat which will soon be filled with heavy water," she began, excitement in her voice. "We'll be going down to see it in a few minutes. Now, when one of the trillions of neutrinos zipping through this vat collides with an electron of our heavy water, it will shoot that electron out of its orbit at a speed greater than the speed of light. This creates the subatomic equivalent of a sonic boom, a little trail of blue light called Cerenkov light, which is picked up on the photomultiplier tube, otherwise known as a PMT. The PMT is like a tiny camera which photographs the light. Then, by acting as a sort of backwards light bulb, it converts the tiny light signal into an electric impulse, which is amplified a hundred million times and relayed to the computers you see here. These state-of-the-art machines are programmed to distinguish the neutrino signals from other background radiation -- which we call "noise" -- that reaches the photomultipliers and must be screened out. Any questions so far?"

"How many neutrinos would be registered in a day?" asked a pink-faced young woman with blond hair.

"The expected number of 'hits' per day is relatively small, from ten to twenty on average," replied Biz.

A short, dark-headed young man with an acne-scarred face spoke up energetically. "Dr. Oliver said that there will be trillions of neutrinos streaming through the vat every second -- how can such a small number be significant?"

Miles had been studying the computer panel and threw a smile at the student to acknowledge the question, then returned to the panel.

Biz replied. "We know from research at particle accelerators that the probability of a neutrino ever interacting with any other subatomic particle is minuscule, approaching zero. You must remember that the neutrino has no charge and that it is virtually without mass. The vast majority would shoot freely through a wall of lead between here and the moon as if they were flying through empty space. The point I am coming to is that we know what the odds are of capturing these little nothings, and even if we can't catch very many, we can tell from the number and the direction and the type that we do catch, a great deal about the universe beyond us.

"Any more questions?" she asked, glancing around at the solemn young faces.

Peter Jones from the Laurentian physics department spoke up. "And how long is the programme expected to run?"

"We hope to keep it running for five years," replied Biz. "That will depend upon government financing. But running it will be cheap compared to the construction phase, which is just finishing now.

"Okay, then," Biz continued, we'll have a look over the side and then we'll take you down below to see the vat that will hold the heavy water."

Biz led the students outside the control room onto the concrete balcony, and leaning over the pipe rail, she pointed down. "It's one helluva long drop," she said soberly. "Take a look -- it's like standing on the roof of a tall building. You can just barely see the light they're working under, way down there at the bottom."

"Spo-o-o-ky," someone whispered.

"Awesome," breathed another.

"I wouldn't want to be stuck down here alone," agreed Biz, continuing with her spiel. "This rugged norite rock has been blasted out to form the gigantic cavity below us..."

Nell stood by the door, a little apart from the group, observing. Jack and Miles Oliver stood beside the rail, and Miles began to explore, moving away from the group and looking down, craning his head as he did so.

Jack wandered off in Miles' direction, standing politely and formally through Biz' presentation, hands clasped behind his back. Miles Oliver straightened up, turned and addressed Suhara.

"How will the heavy water tank be stabilized within the ultrapure?"

"You will see the ropes when we go to the base," replied Suhara tersely. Then, looking at his watch, he caught Biz' eye and motioned that it was time to move on.

"Onwards and upwards," prattled Biz happily, much in her element showing off the observatory. "Or I should have said downwards --I'll turn you over to Mr. Suhara now, who will take

106

you down for the *real* view."

"Follow me and Dr. Oliver, please," requested Suhara politely, as he led the way through the control room and along the spotless painted concrete corridors, which even now were being hosed down. Soon, the men walking as before, they had navigated the steep ramp to the lower level, where Suhara activated the vertical door as Mike had done earlier. Then, along the lower tunnel to the landing, where the double doors to the pit rolled open and Nell was transported once again into the eerie underworld that held the key to the heavens above. This time the enormous dimly lit sphere, completed now but still empty, hung delicately in mid-air from heavy ropes which stretched up to the deck of the control room. Sam Carney was on the telephone to the control room, holding a calculator as he spoke. He smiled at the group and switched on the spotlights -- the photomultiplier tube reflectors glared unblinkingly out of the blackness like the eyes of some gigantic insect, forcing audible gasps from the students.

For the first time, Jack Suhara smiled. "Yes, it is very impressive," he said proudly. "It is a sight very few people will ever see. We finished attaching the photomultiplier tubes only today, and now we are testing the suspension lines for stretch and balance. We are about to lower the sphere back onto this platform, and tomorrow we will begin to fill both the sphere and this cavity." He turned to the doors, pointing. "There are massive metal bulkheads in the rock there, just inside the doors. They will be wound into position and sealed to make the cavity waterproof."

There was silence as the young faces peered into the vault above. One of the lads, face pallid in the underground light, backed into the shadows and turned to face the rock wall. Biz slipped quietly to his side, and Nell could hear her reassuring voice. "Don't worry -- it happens to people sometimes. The cavity is unnatural and people find it shocking. There were miners who couldn't stand it down here -- the size of it made them phobic."

"My knees feel like water," he said, a little shakily.

"What is your name?" asked Biz kindly.

"Martin."

"Come and sit in the trolley, Martin. We'll only be here a few minutes," and as she spoke a delicate wan-faced girl with tears in her eyes came to join them.

Jack Suhara was speaking again. "Tomorrow morning the engineers will test the water delivery system for leaks and in the afternoon the filling process will begin. This must be precisely regulated, so that the heavy-water tank inside that fragile dome of cameras will be floated into the exact centre of its ultrapure bath..."

Nell glanced again at the students. Most were listening to Jack Suhara but the Indonesian boy was still captivated, trance-like, by the immensity above him. Miles Oliver was standing beside the boy, his eyes fixed on the wonder in the young face. His arm came up gently to encircle the slight shoulders. The boy gave a small start, then glanced up at the physics professor and smiled.

"Sir, it really is magnificent! It is a mirror of the heavens, is it not?"

"Indeed it is, my boy," said Miles, pointing up with the other arm. "But don't assume that the mirror is aimed in just the one direction, upwards, like a conventional telescope. The neutrinos are whistling through here from all points of the compass -- up from Indonesia and down from Sudbury. Neutrino events will be recorded from all over the universe."

Suhara had paused to listen and now interrupted his own discourse in a controlled voice. "I hear Dr. Oliver is speaking as well. He says the neutrinos will be coming from all directions, which leads to my next point. Biz told you that the heavy water electrons would be knocked out of orbit to leave a trail of light. In order to photograph the precise angle of these trailing lights, the ten thousand little cameras you see on the dome have been positioned by a computer programme into a perfect sphere. This is what will allow us to compute the directions of neutrinos arriving from all points in the heavens."

Biz approached Jack Suhara and addressed him in a low voice. Suhara nodded. "I had forgotten the time. We are due back up at the surface," and he turned towards the trolley.

Miles was standing between Suhara and the tram and now spoke brightly to Biz. "I'd like a crack at driving that thing! How about if I take you and these two kids and my Indonesian friend up and let Mr. Suhara and the others walk for a change?"

"Fine with me," said Biz, climbing in beside Miles. "37741K."

Miles reached under the dash, entered the code, the doors swung open, and the tram smoothly mounted the track. Nell climbed the hill through the dim tunnel behind the little knot of students, an unhappy Suhara in step beside her.

CHAPTER 14

At 6:45 on Friday evening, Sam Carney, Morgan Washington, and Chuck Farraday climbed wearily out of the tram and summoned the cage. It had been a long grinding day, but the big soccer ball, as they called it, was complete -- suspended now in all its glory a few inches above the construction platform at the base of the pit. Farraday and his crew had worked long hours to meet the deadline on the installation and hook-up of the water lines.

"Damn lift, takes forever," muttered Carney with uncharacteristic irritation.

"What's your problem, Sam?" said Washington. "We're *finished!* It's time to celebrate, man, go out and have some fun!"

Carney opened his mouth to speak, glanced at Farraday, and shut it.

"Come on," said Washington, "let's grab a shower, have a drink, and get us a fine dinner in town."

"Yeah, okay," said Carney flatly, lapsing into silence.

When they reached topside, Farraday took his leave, heading home to his beautiful wife and two young children. Morgan's spirits were irrepressible as he and Carney rolled into Sudbury and parked in front of the steakhouse, where they were soon seated in a comfortable booth.

"Ah've got a date tomorrow," beamed Morgan Washington softly. "With Ms. Modeste -- we're going to the opera!"

"Good for you," replied Carney, opening the menu.

"What *is* it with you tonight?" exclaimed Washington. "You're acting like a caged bear!"

Carney closed the menu with a certain resolve and placed it deliberately on the table, fitting its corner to the corner of the tabletop. "That's it," he said with finality. "I'm calling Cam MacAllister. This whole thing's gotten out of hand."

"What's gotten out of hand?" asked Washington, eyeing the menu.

"The accidents on this project!" declared Carney. "These Canadians are in too big a hurry. Somebody's going to get hurt. Maybe *Cam* will listen to reason!"

"Who would want to do it?" asked Morgan, selecting the prime rib.

"I dunno...I've been too busy to think about it. It's a matter for the police, anyway. It's been going on for months. Remember? My son was suspected over that elevator panel."

"I thought it might have been Suhara," said Washington. "It still might be, but Mike was adamant this morning that Suhara's onside."

"Mike's adamant about a lot," said Sam.

"Well at least he makes decisions -- good ones -- and quick, too. But we'd better keep an eye on Suhara all the same."

The waitress returned, the men ordered their meals, then ate in silence. After dessert, Carney excused himself and went to the telephone.

"Hello?" came Cam's low and level voice.

"Cam? It's Sam Carney. Sorry to bother you at home. How's Nettie?"

"Really good today!" answered Cam, in high spirits. "It was just like old times. I'm going back in the morning. What's up?"

"It's about the accidents on the project. It's awkward, going around Mike, but I need to talk to you. Washington and I confronted him this morning about that return-air switch and it turns out it was pulled deliberately."

There was a pause. "Did he say anything else?"

"He said both he and I knew we weren't going to shut things down while we figured it out. He's upping security and we're to keep it to ourselves."

"The project is due to open Wednesday," thought Cam aloud. "The construction is finished. The crews will be leaving tomorrow..."

111

"It could be anybody!" broke in Carney. "It could be someone on the team! It doesn't matter who it is. The point is it's escalating. If someone gets killed, or if the lab gets wrecked, where will we be then? What in God's name are our priorities?"

"Hold on, Sam! This is really up to Mike, and Siegel. It's their call, not ours."

"It's political -- I know that. We're near the finish line, and they don't want another delay. But they're crazy, they could lose the whole ball of wax! If some madman blows this thing up there'll be hell to pay -- in the news, in the courts, in the science community. Jesus Christ, Cam! *Think* about it!"

"Calm down, Sam! Don't try to panic me." Another pause. "All right, all right. I'll talk to Siegel. Call me back in half an hour."

Surfacing from the underground tour, Nell returned to the office to close up for the day. It was 6:15. She felt uneasy. There was something not quite right that she couldn't put a finger on, something trying to gel that wouldn't. She needed someone to talk to, someone female and intuitive and trustworthy. Biz. Dinner with Biz. But was it safe to leave the project?

She went in to see Mike. He held a strip of pizza in one hand, the other tapped at the keyboard. "Still here?" he asked absently.

"Yes, the students have just left. You working tonight?"

"From now on I'll be glued to this damn place day and night until it opens. No bloody peace for the wicked."

"I'd like to have dinner with Biz," she said.

"She and Kelly usually go out Friday nights," he replied. "They're probably over in one of the trailers. You might catch them."

As Nell approached the trailers through the darkness, the merriment of Friday night happy hour floated out across the snow. She followed the sound of the party to trailer C, tapped on the door, and was greeted enthusiastically by Harry Mintzman, insisting on being called Mintz. His room was larger than her own, boasting a sofa, several easy chairs, and a double bed. Seated around the small room and on the bed were Moira, Carl Hoffman, Hilaire Modeste, Miles Oliver, Biz, Alex Wong, Kelly Rowe, and an affable young man with tightly curled brown hair she had never seen before. The company greeted her with a hail of welcomes, then Carl Hoffman put a friendly arm around her shoulders and led her to a bar on the bathroom counter where a little radio piped out jazz piano. Pouring wine into a tumbler amidst this happy crowd, she felt miles removed from the chilling reality of the attack on the lab.

For once Mintzman and Hoffman were not discussing MSW. Moira was focused on a young man speaking excitedly about Internet search engines. He produced a business card and handed it to her, accepting one in return, an exchange of e-mail addresses. Miles Oliver watched this transaction rather blankly, then stated that on the telephone one could at least hear a human voice, and that he preferred books over computer screens. He looked around for support. Nell smiled and Miles winked at her, adding, "The fax machine serves very well in a pinch."

Nell managed to squeeze in between Biz and Alex Wong, saying she could eat a horse. Biz immediately asked Nell to join her and Kelly for a Greek dinner. "Kalamari? My favourite!" replied Nell. "What's everybody else doing tonight?"

"I'm going home to my family when I finish this beer," said Alex.

"And the rest of this crew is going over to Seafoods North," added Carl Hoffman.

Nell set down her glass and told Biz she was going to her room to freshen up. She went directly to D-7 and knocked. He waved her in and began talking.

"Siegel called back while you were down in the lab," said Robin. "Apparently Hawthorpe has health problems. He's a nervous type, you can see that. He's broken down a couple of times and been hospitalized. He's on medication."

"Where is he now?" she asked.

"He gave his paper on dark matter this afternoon. He looked terrible, wouldn't look in my direction at all. As soon as he finished he excused himself. I followed him out -- he went to his trailer. Haven't seen him since."

"Have you eaten?" asked Nell.

"I've got bagels and cheese," he replied. "I'll be okay. I'm going to keep an eye on Hawthorpe tonight, he's just down the hall here."

113

"Biz and Kelly are waiting for me," said Nell. "We're going to town. Perhaps they'll shed some light. The rest are having seafood somewhere. The Internet guy is here. Mike's working tonight, and Jack came up from the lab with me and went home. He seemed preoccupied. Something was upsetting him down in the mine -- he was quite uncivil to Dr. Oliver."

"No wonder, after this morning. Fuses are getting short. Things should be okay for tonight though -- Mike's here, the night watchman, the pipefitter, and me. Perhaps you should check in later."

"I'll tap on your window," she said, and returned to the party.

Carney and Washington were coming out of the warehouse as the three women crossed to the parking lot.

"Just look at that Morgan Washington!" said Kelly. "He's walking on air! What I wouldn't give to have a man look at me the way he looks at Hilaire Modeste!"

"He's really sweet," agreed Biz, "and it's about time someone treated him right. I hope this works out for him."

"He told me his wife left him and the kids," said Nell.

"Sam Carney knows them. According to him she's a real gold-digger," confirmed Kelly.

What a close-knit community this neutrino team was, thought Nell as she slid into Kelly's car. Perhaps the evening would hold some clues. Kelly drove well. She chose productive lanes, taking Kingsway through town, and soon they were seated in the restaurant.

The women took their time over dinner, enjoying a series of appetizers before the main course. Biz and Kelly's Friday night tradition was well-established. Neither woman was married and each Friday they would select a different restaurant and unwind from the hectic week. Nell was happy in their company, the exchanges quick, witty and upbeat, though they spoke little of the project.

There had been no suitable opening in the conversation by the time the waiter took the dessert order. Nell decided to take the plunge.

She assumed a worried frown. "I hope Mike's in a better mood next week. He's been a real thundercloud the last couple of days, yelling at people, slamming the phone down, storming in and out.

I've been on tenterhooks."

Biz shrugged knowingly. "Oh, don't worry about Mike. He's all bark and no bite. He's very fair, you know. If he gives someone hell they deserve it, believe me."

"Well, he was sure giving it to the Purchasing Commission yesterday. They held up the project with the wrong pipe brackets. Boy, was he mad! He must be stressed, with all the delays they've had."

"Yes," said Kelly, "Mike blows up but when it's over it's over. He doesn't hold grudges. He's one of those people -- you get the clouds and the storm, then the sun comes out and it's all forgotten."

Neither woman was taking the bait on the delays. They were more interested in their attractive, volatile project director. Coffee and baklava arrived at the table. Time was running short.

She tried another tack. "I couldn't believe the cafeteria this morning, the place full of work crews, milling around, waiting for the all-clear. Did you two get caught up in that?"

"Yes!" said Biz. "I was down in the control room with Alex when Chuck Farraday came running in yelling at us to get topside. The fumes didn't reach the control room, it's airtight. But they could have caused an explosion in the pit."

"I was at the conference and missed the excitement," said Kelly, "but I heard the return-air fan broke down."

"Yes, it's an old mine and some of the equipment we use on the project has been causing problems," said Biz. "Alex is always joking about it. Putting high-tech neutrino equipment down a dilapidated mineshaft. But at least we can afford the project -- we could never have built the shaft from square one."

The conversation had veered off a second time, both women apparently innocent of the dilemma Mike and Siegel were facing. She gave it a final try.

"This project has brought some pretty impressive people together. I had no idea when I left Vancouver. But today I had the strangest experience!"

"Oh? What was that?" asked Biz. Both forks paused in mid-air.

"I was out running at lunchtime. I was overtaken by Dr. Kettering..."

"Lucky you!" said Biz. "Isn't he a peach?"

"Yes, he is nice," said Nell, "but that's not it. We were running together along the road, on our way back, when this little blue car shot over the hill behind us and skidded right into us. If Dr. Kettering hadn't hurled me across the ditch I would have been toast!"

"You're *kidding!*" said Kelly, eyes wide. "Who was it?"

"It was Dr. Hawthorpe. And the thing is, he didn't *stop!* Just kept going like a bat out of hell, honking and waving as if nothing had happened!"

Biz was silent a moment, considering whether to speak her mind. "He has his problems," she said. "He's more to be pitied than despised. He's one of those genius-bordering-on-mad people. Brilliant theorist, detached from everyday life -- you know the type."

"Someone should detach him from his driver's licence," fumed Nell. "He's rude, too. Did you hear the way he spoke to Mr. Krishna the other night?"

Kelly spoke up. "He's wired, high strung, like a bird. I've seen him in meetings. He'll get excited and reach for his tranquilizers. He keeps them in his pocket."

"But it's more than that," insisted Nell. "Why didn't he stop to make sure we were all right? To apologize? It's outlandish!"

"This happened at lunchtime?" asked Kelly. "He was late getting back. He had to give a paper. He rushed into the workshop in a panic."

"That doesn't excuse him," said Biz, turning to Nell. "He probably couldn't face you and Dr. Kettering."

"Then he's right off balance," concluded Nell. "I wonder if he's been responsible for any of the..." She checked herself and reached for the tab.

"The what?" asked Kelly.

"Oh, just something Dr. Washington said. Accidents on the project, perhaps deliberate. None of my business though."

"There's been speculation of foul play but no proof," said Biz. "At least not that they're telling us. Most of us have been too busy to give it much thought. What did Dr. Washington say?"

"He was worried about sabotage. Perhaps Jack Suhara." Nell wondered if she was betraying a confidence.

"Jack? *Jack?*" repeated Kelly in disbelief. *"Who's* unbalanced?

116

How could Morgan suggest such a thing? Jack is the most committed, fastidious guy in the place! He works lunches, evenings..."

"That would give him opportunity," mused Biz. "But that's crazy! I agree with Kelly, he works super hard –funny though – my boss Alex doesn't like him, doesn't seem to trust him. I can't figure it out. Alex is so easy going."

Nell made a mental note to talk to Alex, then said, "Well who else around here would want to botch things up?"

Kelly frowned. "My bet is that *if* someone's up to no good, it's not one of the team -- and certainly not Hawthorpe, however bad his nervous system. He's too keen on the results. You have to remember, these are all seasoned people, they've been on the heels of the neutrino problem for years. Cam has the Nobel prize, Miles is up for a knighthood, Sam and Moira are tops in their fields, and most of the others are full professors and department heads. If someone has an axe to grind, it's a grudge of some sort, and most of the extra people will be out of here tomorrow."

"Amen!" said Biz, winking at Nell. "Kelly and I made a rule. We don't talk shop on Friday nights. Self defence. Now, are we in the mood for karaoke?"

Nell gave up. Why not take their lead and relax for a change? "Sure thing! Let's do the town!"

The waitress brought back Sam Carney's American Express card and informed him there was a telephone call waiting for him from a Mr. Siegel.

Sam, having vented his feelings to MacAllister, and with a bellyful of good wine and steak, was now more subdued. Doubt tugged at his mind as he walked to the telephone.

"Carney here."

"Sam, we did meet once, I believe. It's Ed Siegel. I understand you're concerned about the safety of our project. Let me assure you that we are taking every precaution to ensure that nothing more will happen."

"If you're taking every precaution, how the hell did someone get into the utility room to pull that switch?" Sam argued, confidence returning.

117

"Be fair now," replied Siegel. "We had no idea until that happened how determined our man is. I spoke to the Minister, told him there was a security problem, and he said to get some professional undercover help. We've done that, it's the pipefitter. He's got a cot in the warehouse."

"It's an *insider,*" protested Carney. "He can't stop our own people from going down there to work! Why is it any safer today than it was yesterday?"

"Because all the attempts have been on the surface, which points to someone on the team," said Siegel slowly.

Carney paused. "Any member of the team has access to the lab, and if he's determined he'll use it."

"As of this morning, no one goes down alone," said Siegel. "There is still a risk, but it's more acceptable. It does not make sense to create panic this close to opening. And delaying at the last minute to investigate will not ensure that we catch our man, who could strike any time in the future."

For Carney it was a losing battle. Siegel had the will and the logic of a powerful man. But there was one more point. "Our saboteur seems to want to delay the opening," he said. "He may make an all-out effort now, and then if he fails, quit trying."

"We are taking that possibility into account. Now if you have no further objections, we will proceed with the filling of the tanks this weekend, and the computer hook-ups on Monday and Tuesday. I know you will respect our decision in this matter and keep your counsel."

"If I'm going to stay on the project I have no choice," replied Sam with a touch of bitterness. "That's about it, then."

"I appreciate your concern," said Siegel. "If you see anything at all suspicious, please report it to the pipefitter."

Kelly and Biz returned Nell to the project at 11:15 and waited until old Harry came to unlock the gate before driving off singing into the night. Nell went to trailer "D" and tossed a small stone against the darkened pane. Instantly the window opened. He held a finger to his lips and motioned her around into the trailer. "Nothing new," whispered Nell, slipping into his room. "They think someone on the work crew has a grudge."

The bedside light was on now and he was in casual dress, barefoot. Probably catching a wink while keeping watch, she thought, her eyes drawn to his feet and ankles. Thoroughbred.

"Possibly. It isn't Hawthorpe." He motioned her to the chair.

"How do you know?"

"I went to see him. After what Siegel said, and the way he looked this afternoon, I thought he might go over the edge. I knocked on his door about 7:30. The TV was on, but no answer. I knocked louder. Still nothing. I went around to the window and there he was, slumped over his laptop. There was a bottle of pills on the table..."

"He wasn't *dead!*"

"It looked like it, but when I banged on the window he stirred a little. I jimmied the lock with my penknife and crawled in and managed to bring him around. I got him to retch into the sink, then poured black coffee down him while he lay there propped up on the pillows, docile and subdued. Finally he gave a great sigh and began to talk."

"Attempted suicide?"

"He didn't say. But he's had a bad time. It's been going on for years. Pervasive anxiety. Once he started to tell me about it he was quite human.

"He went down to the project alone today," Robin continued, "just out of curiosity. He'd taken his medication this morning but the excitement of seeing it began to get to him on the way up. His hands were shaking as he tried to open the pills and he dropped them. The container bounced on the floor, then through the bars of the cage and down the shaft into oblivion. He had to give his paper at 2:00 but was in no condition to do it, so he rushed into town for a prescription. He was late coming back, going too fast, and he hit the brakes when he saw us. The near-miss finished him off and he panicked."

"How utterly embarrassing."

"He was aghast at himself. Mortified. He could hardly get through his presentation and went straight to his room afterwards. The whole misery of the last few years caved in on him and the evening news was just too much. A serial rapist. Ireland. Africa. Israel. North Korea. He swallowed a handful of pills and sat down at the laptop to write an apology to his wife..."

119

"My God! And we had him down as a murderer!"

"We're back to square one," said Robin wearily.

Nell stood up. "Not quite square one, Robin. At least Hawthorpe is eliminated. Perhaps he'll feel better in the morning. He's got it off his chest now, thanks to you -- you handled that like a pro."

"D'ya think so?" he brightened.

"I sure do!" and she slipped quietly out of the trailer.

CHAPTER 15

Nell awoke early Saturday into a well of loneliness. She had dreamed vividly of Patrick. For some time she lay very still in the narrow bed, holding her breath against the return of grief.

They had met in her little bookstore down on Fourth Avenue and had on several charming occasions enjoyed animated and comfortable conversations. After each such occasion Nell would feel a glow of happiness during the hours and evening that followed.

There had been a deep shyness between them that did not permit either to move the friendship beyond the rather fragile delight that each took in the other's company. But Nell had always been aware of an almost palpable sphere of radiant warmth surrounding Patrick whenever they stood together in the store.

One late November evening he came into the bookstore near closing time and told her that he was going to move to Australia. She had turned quickly away to protect her face from observation as the force of the disappointment overwhelmed her.

She remembered that she had borrowed a book from him and excused herself momentarily, then moved around past him and through the curtains into the back of the shop to fetch it. A desperate excitement played over and into her limbs. She picked up the slender volume and glanced through the curtains at his standing frame as he concentrated his attention upon a book. A solid, but not heavy man, well-knit angular bones apparent through sweater and corduroys. There was a suchness to his being that she had always marvelled at, a magnified sentience that set him apart.

The excitement was growing with restless urgency, driven by a sense of impending loss, a now-or-never pang of fear. She walked over to him with the book in both hands and in his glance and in his thanks she saw a mirror of her own questioning uncertainty.

"I've got to run," he said, almost apologetically, and with a quick shy smile left the store.

Nell was frantic. She looked at her watch, 4:57. Closing in three minutes. She hurriedly locked the till, collected her purse and coat, and turned out the lights.

She stepped out into the wet November street and locked the shop. She turned towards the supermarket parking lot where he always left his car. It was gone. In a frenzy she scanned the intersection for it, thinking to run up and tap on the window, anything, anything, to let him know. She caught a fleeting glance of the old Chrysler as it turned the corner up ahead.

She stood, almost swaying, in the shadow of an awning for a minute or two, in a state of excited yet not unwelcome anguish, a strange compelling restlessness upon her.

A figure moved in the darkness behind her, she half-turned to let the stranger pass. In turning she just had time to recognize him as his outstretched arms engulfed her and she sank into that solid warmth, her self fusing into it, indistinguishable from it, her own distant voice repeating, "Oh...oh...oh...oh..." as the embrace overtook her, flooding her universe with ultimate sweetness.

Now, Nell, lying in this trailer bed, wept for that lost love, their own shared treasure, nearly twice-lost, such a risk had it been to declare.

Presently her thoughts returned to the project. It was discouraging not knowing whom to trust, though now there was a sanctuary in Robin, who in some strange way had been connected to the dream. Her energy was at a low ebb; she had no wish to get up or to see anyone. But she did what she had to -- arose dispiritedly and dressed for the day.

She entered the administration building through the cafeteria. It was only 8:15. Odd, Mike's truck was not in the parking lot.

She ordered eggs and coffee and took them along to the office. Mike's door to the hallway was shut but through it came a woman's voice. Quietly she entered her adjoining office, leaving the light out and placing the eggs in a drawer to contain the aroma.

She crept over to Mike's door and put an ear up to it. Once again, she was eavesdropping on Moira.

"I know how much you respect him, darling, he's brave and he stands alone..."

A large truck came rumbling into the yard outside, drowning out the words. Nell took the opportunity to pick up the receiver on Mike's line and listen in.

A soft, intent, childlike voice. "Mom, he's right, he's right! You *know* he's right! Those neutrinos just aren't there. The whole model is obsolete and I want the world to know."

"It may or may not be obsolete, Evan. But you're taking a *terrible risk!* There are thousands of dollars at stake, perhaps millions. If you're wrong it's the game that will be obsolete!"

"I'm willing to take that risk, Mom -- it's my call, I invented it..."

"But darling, if you lose, you'll be back where you started -- no meaning in your life, no confidence, no future..."

"He gives me confidence, Mom, and he's proved to me why the standard model is wrong. I *can't* let him down!"

"He's a father figure to you, which is wonderful, but his science is flawed."

"It isn't! Yes, I love him like a father, and I respect his mind as well. I'm going through with it," said the boy with finality.

"Damn!" said Moira in exasperation. "I wish to God they'd never built this project and then it wouldn't matter!"

"Another project would prove it sooner or later," Evan said reasonably. "I'll talk to you later, Mom. Don't worry, it'll work out."

"Just *wait* a few months, until we get some counts..."

"Can't! Gotta go, Mom. Thanks for calling."

Moira sighed audibly. "Goodbye, darling," and hung up.

Nell quickly replaced the receiver and straightened up to turn on the light and retrieve the eggs.

A moment later there was a knock at the door. Moira

123

appeared in an elegant jumpsuit.

"Good morning," she said with a rather tense smile. "I didn't realize you were here."

"Just came in," said Nell, reaching for her cup. "Can I help you?"

"No, that's all right. I didn't think Mike would mind if I used his phone -- I had to call my son."

"I'm sure he wouldn't mind."

"I wonder what time he'll be in?" inquired Moira.

This was odd, thought Nell. Surely Moira knew that Mike was on the project day and night. But where was he this morning? Perhaps they had spent the night together and were covering up. None of her business anyway.

"He should be in pretty soon. They're going to be testing the water system this morning."

"I'll wait," said Moira, picking up a magazine and taking it into Mike's office, closing the door behind her.

Nell was seated in front of the computer idly waiting for it to boot when the unsettled feeling she had experienced yesterday coming up from the mine returned with force. Now it dawned clearly that a number of people found the laboratory to be an unnatural and disturbing place. Two of the students had been unnerved by it, and some of the miners had found that giant cavity just too large to be that far down in the earth...

Biz and Kelly had put the project's delays down to accidental mishaps, or at most to a grudge. With sudden excitement, Nell opened the personnel directory on her computer, then scanned the date-ordered files for links to August 8th, September 6th, and October 3rd. One of the entries was dated August 8th, a Thursday. Marty Roark, miner. She opened the file. Marty had been drilling and bolting the cavity roof to ensure stability. He had resigned Monday August 5th. Reason given: the excavation was too dangerous. He had come in late Thursday afternoon to pick up his last check.

It seemed to fit. Nell checked the September and October dates: none of the personnel files had been actioned at those times.

She looked in the telephone directory. There it was, Roark, Marty-Jenny. Nell followed a hunch. She dialled the number. A young female voice came on the line, clear and quiet.

"Good morning," said Nell in a cheerful, businesslike tone. "Is that Mrs. Roark?"

"Yes."

"My name is Mary Stockwell and I'm doing a research paper on employment issues in the Sudbury area. Would you have a few minutes to answer some questions?"

"Unemployment? That's a problem for some of us...is this a telephone survey? How long will it take?"

"It's an academic survey. About five minutes," said Nell. "The questions are easy."

"Okay. Go ahead."

"Is anyone in your household out of work now, or been laid off during the last six months?"

"Well, my husband's out of work but he wasn't laid off -- he quit his mining job back in August. He's in Labrador now, looking for work."

"Oh!" said Nell, with surprise. "How am I going to record that? Voluntary severance?"

"Well no, he didn't want to quit, he had to. It was that awful science project, that huge underground pit. He couldn't stand it. It gave him nightmares. He thought it would cave in on him..."

"How terrible!" said Nell. "I'll put it down as health reasons."

"Well, he wasn't actually sick," said Jenny. "He was afraid, because he thought the cavern was too big to take the pressure from the mile of rock above it. He said it was eerie down there, a hazard to the miners. Marty talked to the foreman about it, but he wouldn't do anything."

"I'm sorry your husband's out of work," said Nell. "I hope he can find something in Labrador."

"Yes, but then we'd have to move...is that all?" asked Jenny.

"Are you or anyone else in your home unemployed?" asked Nell.

"I work at the dry cleaner's, and my father, who's living with us now, is retired."

"Shall I mark you down as full-time, then?"

"Yes, thank heaven! Tuesday to Saturday. I have to go now."

"Thanks very much for your time, Mrs. Roark."

Marty had talked to Farraday, then. Farraday was scheduled

to help Mike and the engineers with the water lines this morning. Nell went to the cafeteria to look out to the parking lot and spotted the two men pulling up in Mike's truck. She was paying for coffee as they came in.

"Morning Nell," said Mike. "I went to get Chuck."

"Wife needed the car this morning," said Chuck proudly. "Took the boy to his hockey game."

Nell grinned at Chuck and made a stick handling motion. "Moira's waiting to see you, Mike. Chuck, do you remember a Marty Roark? Someone wants a reference."

"Oh sure, I remember Marty. Nice guy. Terrified of the hole, though. The best guy to ask would be Wally Robb, he worked with Marty on the roof. He's in the phone book."

Nell returned to the office and put the second cup of coffee next to the first. She found the number and dialled.

"Is that Mr. Robb? This is Nell Fitzgerald from the Canadian Neutrino Project. We've been asked for a reference for Marty Roark. I understand you worked with him."

"Yeah, he was good -- would have worked out fine, except he didn't trust the engineers. Thought it was too dangerous, took things into his own hands. The depths do funny things to people. I can't really recommend him for underground. Maybe someplace above, not below. Okay?"

"How d'ya mean, took things into his own hands? What did he do?"

"Well, between you and me, he trashed that elevator panel -- trying to protect his buddies from a rockburst. No need to repeat that, though. Just say he works better up top."

"Was there anybody down there?"

"What? Oh, no. It was around dinner time. No one below."

"Thanks for your candour. By the way, have you seen him lately?"

"Last I saw him was a coupl'a weeks after he quit. We had a few beer, that's when he told me about the elevator. He was feelin' bad about it. Left town looking for work."

"Thanks, Mr. Robb. Appreciate your help."

Progress. Old Hernandez had been on the project August 8th but had obviously not inspired the attack on the elevator. No one on the science team had been pushed to extremes, not that day.

But why had the project been delayed three times since, and most particularly, why this past Thursday night?

The telephone rang, interrupting her thoughts.

"I've had trouble getting through." It was Siegel.

"Sorry. I've been doing some sleuthing," and she told him the Roark story, leaving out the name for Jenny's sake. According to the personnel files it looked like an isolated incident.

"One mystery solved," he said, "and three spring up in its wake. Perhaps it gave someone ideas."

"That's possible," said Nell. "We've eliminated Hawthorpe, though," and she relayed Robin's story of the night before.

"Poor Hawthorpe. Well, you're narrowing it down, Mrs. O'Donovan, but it's still very dangerous. Here's something else. Last night Cam MacAllister called me, quite perplexed. Sam Carney had just been on the phone to him, shocked by the sabotage -- he wanted to close the lab down. So does Bridges. I told Cam I'd handle it and called Carney back myself. It took some time but I managed to calm him down. Both Cam and I are under pressure from the Minister to open on time. I spoke to the Minister and he will not begin a formal investigation on the project this close to opening. That leaves the ball in my court, and I still believe our best chance is Dr. Kettering's idea of baiting our man with new-age physics. The trap we lay tomorrow morning with Siddhu Krishna may flush him out."

"Our perpetrator might not attend the talk."

"His absence would make him conspicuous," he countered.

"Are we assuming he's male?"

"No, we're not -- just a manner of speaking," replied Siegel.

"Robin and I will both be there," said Nell thoughtfully. "And afterwards the team will be touring down below. I suppose whoever it is might try then."

"Indeed they might, though it is unlikely our perpetrator would risk his or her own neck. Remember that all attempts to date have been made from the surface. Keep your eyes peeled, Mrs. O'Donovan, and take no chances. I want to return you to your Gulf Island in one piece!"

It was 10:30 now and the office was quiet. Robin had taken some of the team into town to get car rentals for the weekend. Mike had been outside with the test tanker and came into the office to warm up. He stood redfaced in the doorway in his sheepskin coat, rubbing his hands vigorously and banging his feet.

"Do you have a minute?" she asked, remembering Moira's telephone call.

"Just one," he said gruffly. "What is it?"

Nell recounted the telephone conversation she had heard between Moira and Evan while Mike waited impatiently, nodding his head and signalling her to bring it to a close.

"Yeah, I know all that."

Nell was exasperated. "Why in God's name am I tracking this woman if you already know her position? Why didn't somebody *tell* me?"

Mike smiled at this show of pique, then sobered.

"Can you keep a secret?" he asked seriously.

"Just one."

"All right. One time when the team was meeting here, it was right after Moira's husband had killed himself. She was holding up pretty well, but she drank too much. She started to lose it. She was sitting in a corner in the dining lounge with her head turned away and a hand over her eyes. I went over and asked if I could take her outside for a cup of coffee."

He paused, considering whether to continue.

"Did she go?" asked Nell.

"I took her into my office and asked her to wait while I got the coffees, but she just broke down right then and there and the whole story came out."

Nell was about to ask what the secret was, then remembered the back room.

"So you were her shoulder to cry on?"

"Yeah," he said, glancing up a little ruefully. "Somehow the pain in her brought us together."

"But that was some time ago."

"Yeah, but since then I talk to her now and again. She knows I'm married -- she knows I love Penny. But we were close that once so she sometimes talks to me about her son."

"Did she tell you she'd had a tete-a-tete with Dr. Hernandez at midnight in the photomultiplier shop?"

Bridge looked surprised. "No. When was that?"

"The first night, Wednesday. I listened in. It was the same thing, trying to get Hernandez to back off with her son."

"Well she's in a bit of a spot, isn't she? I'll admit she's got motive, but I would be very, very surprised if Moira would try to wreck the..."

"Somebody's sure trying! And Moira said she'd wished to God they'd never built it."

"All right, all right. I'll tell Jack to keep an eye on her."

"Jack?"

"Yeah, he's been playing watchdog on the q.t. I'll be seeing Moira for lunch. She'll probably spill it all then."

Bridges looked at his watch and scowled. "Was that everything?"

Nell nodded. Bridges, disgruntled now, trudged through the snow to the warehouse, shaking his head in disbelief over Moira the saboteur.

CHAPTER 16

"So how many people are coming?" asked Zack, fitting the cable from the LCD panel to the laptop.

"Let me think," answered Nell, as she struggled to balance the ancient screen on its tripod in front of the blackboard. "The engineers are still out there, filling the tank..."

Zack made a wry face. "Filling a *tank?* When they could be surfing the web, clicking the links? Where are their priorities?"

Nell laughed. "They're on a tight schedule, working round the clock. I'm sure if they had a choice they'd be in here where the action is!"

"Who else isn't coming?"

"The skiers," said Nell. "Some of them already surf the 'net so they're skiing the landscape instead. It's a fine day out there!"

"Opted for physical reality over virtual, huh?"

"They've had two full days of workshops," she replied. Though his manner was playful, he needed reassurance.

Zack mounted the LCD panel above the overhead projector, connected the modem, and turned on the laptop. He began busily tapping keys and after a few moments Netscape appeared on the movie screen that Nell had put up.

"Everything's working," said Zack with satisfaction. "Now how many chairs do we need?"

"Me, Hilaire Modeste, Hoffman and Mintzman. That's four. Kelly's coming in, so is Alex, that's six. If Hawthorpe makes it, that's seven. Oh, Mr. Krishna and Robin will probably arrive in later, that's nine."

"Who's Robin? Who's Mr. Krishna?"

"Robin's Dr. Kettering, from the Department of Religious Studies at UBC. He's gone skiing. And Mr. Krishna is the most amazing old Buddhist, you'll love him. He's into consciousness, like Robin. They're friends."

"Then we'll try to do some consciousness links," said Zack.

"Robin will shoot himself for coming late!" said Nell. "Actually he was torn between this and the skiing." Robin and Nell had decided to split up in order to keep tabs on everyone. Moira, Biz, Miles Oliver, and Robin made up the skiing party.

The group began drifting in about 1:20, Mr. Krishna sparkling with energy after his stay in the woods. A chagrined Hawthorpe was the last to arrive. Robin had looked in on him early in the morning and had found him too groggy to join the group going to town for breakfast. As a diversion from the night before he had urged Hawthorpe to attend the Internet session. Hawthorpe, entering the room now, nodded apologetically to Nell, who crossed the room to give him the course manual.

Alex and Kelly were sitting together, perusing their manuals as they waited for Zack. In passing, Nell leaned over Kelly and said, "That was great fun last night at the karaoke bar!" Kelly brightened, then glanced quickly at Alex, who was frowning into his manual. Nell returned to the front of the room and introduced Zack Meyer.

"Thank you, Mrs. Fitzgerald. Okay, let's get going -- time flies like an arrow and fruit flies like a banana..."

Chuckles from Mintz and Hoff, and a "what?" from Hawthorpe.

Zack then questioned his audience re their familiarity with the Web – most used e-mail but some did not use the Internet.

"What is the Internet?" he continued. "Very simply, it's like a humungus spider web which joins together all the computers in the world that want to be joined together. Or, it's like a mega switchboard that connects computers rather than voices. But there's no central switchboard, just a large number of computer addresses that we try to keep a handle on in various ways.

"You've all heard about surfing the 'net, cruising the information highway, crawling the web. We'll be doing that in a few minutes, but first let me explain, for those who are new to it, what is happening when you sign onto the 'net."

He flicked a switch and Netscape came up on the screen. "This page puts a face on the Internet for us, allows us to roam around in computers all over the world. Each computer that we access is called a website. Netscape allows us to browse through text and photographs and even moving pictures that people have mounted on their computers for us to view. But in order to use Netscape, our own computer must first be connected to a telephone or a cable. The telephone is used to dial up a local computer-type switchboard which will connect us to the websites on the information highway. This local switchboard is called the 'Internet provider' and it's your on-ramp and off-ramp to the stream of information -- the highway -- which is moving all the time over telephone lines between computers all over the world. Now is that simple, or what?"

Mintz waved a hand in the air, then spoke up. "Zack, I'm Harry Mintzman. Listen, if you can look into another guy's computer, wouldn't you be able to access all his files, or mess with his data?"

"A common question," said Zack. "No, it doesn't work that way. When you put up a website, and anybody can, it's like publishing a brochure with your ideas, hobbies, products, poems, or whatever you wish to share. The front page of your website -- called your home page -- is like the title page in a book, with a list of contents that the reader can select by clicking the mouse. But before you can put up a website, you must first translate the contents of your brochure or book into a special network language called HTML. There's no way that anyone could access your regular computer files by visiting your website because it's cocooned in this special language."

Mintz persisted. "That's good to know, but I still hear a lot about hacks getting into people's computers and messing around..."

"That's different," replied Zack. "If you work in a shared environment, say in an office on a local area network, then it's possible that someone could find out your e-mail password and break into your work files with it."

"Yeah, at the University they make us change our passwords every month," said Mintz.

"Right...now let's see what lies in store for today. Has anyone a special interest we can try?"

Siddhu Krishna was fast off the mark. "Sir," he began in his deliberate way, "could we look for a website on the physics of consciousness?"

Zack was a little taken aback by the precise speech and austere manner of this gentleman. "Physics of consciousness?" he echoed doubtfully. "We'll try one of the search engines." The keys clacked uner his fingers and up came a page called Google.

"This is a big search engine in the United States," said Zack. "It regularly scans the Internet websites and downloads index words and phrases into its own ginormous database."

Zack positioned the cursor in the searchbox and typed in "physics of consciousness", then waited briefly while the mega-processor zipped through the world's websites to do his bidding.

"Aha!" said Zack. "It's hard to stump Google! Look at that!" and he scrolled through a long list of contents.

"Now," said Zack. "Each item on this list is just the description and address of a computer website that contains information on the physics of consciousness. The list shows that many people out there are so interested in the topic that they have actually mounted their ideas for everyone to share. Each of these items is 'clickable' -- meaning that if I put the mouse on the description and click, Netscape will automatically dial the computer's address and dump me into the website." Then, turning to Mr. Krishna, "Sir, is there one here that especially interests you?"

Siddhu was sitting forward in his chair, enthralled as a child. "Yes," he said. "Please, choose 'my favorite physics and psychology sites', second from the bottom."

Zack clicked and a moment later up came another home page, this one listing dozens more websites. Physics and mind, physics and religion, physics and God -- endless sites offered up by humanity, each with links to further sites, and those in turn to more, stretching infinitely through the collective brain of the planet.

Nell, marvelling at the implications, felt awe as the enormity of this human connectedness washed over her like a benign wave. Anyone and everyone could join in, a living library, evolving minute by minute -- instantaneous, fluid, and democratic, with literacy the only prerequisite.

Krishna flashed his smile at her and commented simply, "In five years it will be as ubiquitous as the telephone."

"Maybe sooner!" beamed Zack. "The cynics say the world is divided in two, those who will use the Internet and those who will not. Most of these people simply have not *seen* it."

Nell wondered about Hawthorpe and looked over. There he sat, naturally and unpretentiously, all defences down, delighted. "Can you go back to the searchbox and put in 'grand unification theory'?"

Zack typed away and once again the network exploded -- with photographs, formulas, book reviews, music, scientific articles, bibliographies -- each with further links to an infinite trail of resources. A sense of excitement and optimism seemed to pervade the entire network. It was like a frontier, thought Nell; this is just the beginning, we have no idea where it will lead.

Hawthorpe kept saying, "Stop, stop, let me get that down!" but Zack just laughed and pushed the bookmark button, which automatically recorded the desired website addresses for future contact.

"Notice," said Zack, "that on many of these physics sites, by simply clicking on an e-mail address you can write to the website's owner. You can have online debates, order products, buy airline tickets, even do your income tax on it -- the possibilities are endless!"

"How about some humour?" asked Carl Hoffman.

"No problem at all." A brief flurry of typing and a click of the mouse produced the website, "Humour with propriety and without". A short story filled the screen.

A young couple, very attracted to each other, was driving along in his convertible on a fine sunny day. "Let's pull off to the side of the road and do it," said the boy. "You can't be serious," objected the girl. "People will be able to see into the car." All right, then," said the boy, pulling the car off the road onto an incline. "We'll get under the car and I'll leave my feet showing a little and if anyone comes along I'll say I'm fixing my muffler." So they wriggled in under the convertible and were just beginning to make love when the boy felt someone kicking his feet. "And just what do you think you're doing?" asked the policeman. "I'm fixing my muffler," declared the young man. "Well you should have fixed your brakes first because your car just rolled down the hill."

"That's good!" roared Hoffman.

"We'll print it," said Zack, and he handed it to Hoffman for future reference.

Mintz asked Zack to search "MSW oscillations" and Nell's enjoyment faded as she was brought back to the neutrino debate and the evil that lurked on the project. When MSW had been explored and the information downloaded for printing, she spoke up.

"I have a completely different sort of question, Zack. Can you test the 'net for moral and philosophic questions, like the origins of good and evil?"

"Oh sure!" he bubbled. "Anything, anything at all. Ask away."

"Okay, how about the source of evil?" Nell glanced around the room a trifle apologetically, adding, "A friend of mine is writing a thesis."

While Zack typed in the search, Nell examined the company present. No one seemed surprised or perturbed. It was like any other question. She checked the time, it was just after four. Hours had evaporated as if they were minutes! The door opened then, and Sam Carney entered the room, followed by Robin and Miles Oliver. Robin scanned the room, smiled at Hawthorpe, and pulled up three chairs next to Nell. Miles sat beside Nell and whispered behind his hand. "These two rogues have strong-armed me into this wretched demonstration. Surely it's almost over?"

Before she could answer, Zack was speaking again. "Here we are. It starts with a website on Carl Gustav Jung. Good and evil." He scrolled down. There were dozens -- hundreds -- of websites. "Can you narrow that down a bit, Mrs. Fitzgerald?"

"Nell...yes. The roots of human evil," she replied, considering. "Ask it about the devil."

"The inner or the outer?" said Robin with a wink.

135

Sam Carney sensed the undercurrent and spoke out. "The devil who would destroy knowledge."

Zack clicked on a Jung page and up came a passage.

"The view that good and evil are spiritual principles outside us, and that man is caught in the conflict between them is more bearable by far than the insight that the opposites are the ineradicable and indispensable preconditions of all psychic life, so much so that life itself is guilt." (Mysterium Coniunctionis, 1955, CW 14, page 266.)

There was a sharp exhale of breath from Hawthorpe, almost a groan. "My dream!" he shouted. "Last night. My body was rolled out flat, like a huge battlefield, and on it the forces of evil and darkness raged, their swords flashing, against my light."

"The light was yours," asked Robin, "but not the dark?"

"I see," said Hawthorpe. "They both belong to me. And to every man. But how utterly strange to read this today!"

"Synchronicity," said Robin, smiling. "Meaningful coincidence between the inner and outer worlds, with no apparent cause."

"Remarkable," said Carl Hoffman.

Hawthorpe resumed, more quietly now. "The statement up there on the screen is true for me. I sank into the depths of despair before I would look at this truth. But through it I have learned that I am the embodiment of conflict, and guilt as well."

"Then you are able to feel," said Hilaire Modeste. "Feeling life includes love and joy, as well as despair and guilt."

Hawthorpe looked over at Hilaire and said, without much conviction, "Yes, I suppose so."

Siddhu Krishna addressed Zack. "Perhaps you have a -- what do you call it -- a home page, on Krishnamurti's view of evil?"

Zack, worried that group therapy was threatening to take over his session, instantly attacked the keyboard. The result appeared with lightning speed.

"All authority of any kind, especially in the field of thought and understanding, is the most destructive, evil

136

thing. Leaders destroy the followers and followers destroy the leaders. You have to be your own teacher and your own disciple. You have to question everything that man has accepted as valuable, as necessary."

"Why this is absurd!" said Miles Oliver. "And dangerous! Our society and social achievements are *grounded* in expertise and authority. Our language, our government, our technology...our transportation, communications, medicine...this Internet should be controlled, censored. I knew it before I came in," and he began to rise from his chair.

Robin spoke. "With all due respect, Dr. Oliver, our social achievements are grounded in the original human genius and vision which were invested in their creation. Authority was an overlay. It came later."

"Authority is our means of keeping order in society and transferring knowledge from one generation to the next," said Miles with a note of finality. "Now if you will excuse me, I have some editing to do."

Hawthorpe stared at the door that Miles Oliver had closed behind him, then looked back at Zack and said, "Well, this is interesting -- I feel rather light -- I'm *learning* something! What else have you got in your bag of tricks?"

Zack laughed and said, "How about a discussion on censorship? Or, if we already support freedom of expression, shall we pay a visit to the Louvre? Or read this morning's London Times? Or check the hockey scores?" and without waiting for a reply he returned to his keyboard.

CHAPTER 17

Dr. Morgan Washington carefully applied the French cologne to his clean-shaven face, then pulled on a starched white shirt and twisted the cufflinks into place. Sliding into the silk suit he smiled satisfaction at the finely-cut garment reflecting back at him from the trailer mirror. Underneath the silk, and behind the mirror's smile, his blood vibrated with longing.

In another trailer, Hilaire Modeste stepped gracefully out of the steaming shower. Rivulets of water ran down her marble litheness from her long pale hair. Turning, an image of beauty unexpectedly revealed itself in the mirror, then shyness demurred from this impression of self and she turned away. Over this shyness, the mirror's impression had evoked a low hum of excitement, a breathless anticipation of the unknown secrets which lay ahead.

Nell lay awake. Outside, the steady drone of the tankers pumping their precious cargo into the cavern below was both comforting and unsettling. The drone seemed to connect her to a darkness, a desperate intent, that shared this very moment yet sought to extinguish its inexorable sound of progress.

I must get into *that* mind, she thought. *I must find a way to destroy this observatory, once and for all.*

She immersed herself in the drone, in the dread of it. She closed her eyes to visualize.

The tankers were pumping life blood into the vastness below, the long arteries bearing the liquid through the subterranean darkness to the enormous heart deep in the earth. The heart lay still -- filling...filling...awaiting fullness and the start of life.

The image ended there. She opened her eyes. The analogy was incomplete. A heart circulated blood, it didn't just receive it. It used veins and arteries, but in this case two arteries led towards the heart, transporting different fluids...

Nell shot bolt upright in bed. *"Confuse* the fluids!" she said aloud. *"Change the caps!"*

What better disaster for the project than to mix up the heavy water with the ultrapure? It would spell the end! The heavy water had been the most costly component of the whole endeavour; there was no way it could be replaced.

The two parallel water lines which Nell had seen with Jack Suhara, one black, the other white, emerged from the parking lot side of the warehouse, each with a screw cap matching its own colour. Each cap was attached to its respective pipe with a short cable. Nell had seen the pipefitter explaining the black and white codes to the truckers earlier in the day. If the cap attachments were changed during the night, it was unlikely that the truckers would notice the discrepancy of colour between the caps and the short lengths of pipe extending from the warehouse.

Suddenly the drone stopped. After a few moments the truck's diesel roared to life and receded out of the compound.

Silence. The tankers were alternating their cargoes. How long would it be before the next truck lumbered into the yard with its alternate fill of water? Nell pulled on her sweat-suit, coat and boots and crept out the back end of the trailer, circling around behind the warehouse and up to the pipe ends on the side of the building, near the front. She peered closely at the caps. They matched their pipes all right, but she noticed that their little cables could be switched with a screwdriver.

What to do? Warn the pipefitter? And tip him off, in the process, that she was undercover too? How much did he know?

Now the sound of a quieter engine, not a diesel, carried across the quiet night from the parking lot. Nell took refuge behind a nearby pile of old photomultiplier crates. Presently the couple emerged into view, walking lazily, arm in arm, heads bent

139

together in languid intimacy.

They stopped in front of the warehouse and turned to one another, her back to Nell. Morgan Washington gently lifted Hilaire's chin and stroked the pale hair from the side of her face. Then, taking her to himself with a slow reverence, he bent to softly brush his lips against her face and mouth.

Nell, touched by Washington's gentleness, but uncomfortable in the role of voyeur, sank back behind the crates and waited.

Presently Washington spoke. "Oh, Hilaire, I'm so in love with you! There is nothing on earth I want more than to be with you tonight. But Ah'm still a married man."

A little sound of anguish rose from Hilaire, almost a sob. "But when *ever* will we be together?" she asked, her voice small, childlike.

"We will have a lifetime together, my love. But it will begin properly, with freedom, with no ties. In the meantime, we will be happy. We will write, we will telephone, and you will never, ever be out of my thoughts."

Hilaire took his face in both her hands and said with that same childlike clarity, "Morgan, I love you with all my heart. I will wait."

They turned to walk, arm in arm, towards the trailers. Nell was touched, taken aback by this glimpse of a mature and selfless reciprocal love. It still existed, if only in real life.

A few minutes later, Morgan Washington returned with a flashlight, checked the pipe caps, then went in to rouse the pipefitter, who had not been alert enough to catch him in the act of examining them.

Nell returned to her trailer, got into bed to warm up and think. Washington, even under the spell of love, had addressed the same concern she had felt. Things seemed to be under control now; he had advised the pipefitter. She fell away into a deep sleep.

Suddenly she came wide awake. She strained to hear the echo of a noise, any trigger for the break from sleep. Nothing. Silence.

That must be it, the drone had quit. But wait. Some half-remembered noise had roused her, some nearby noise; it's shadow clung to her waking mind. She checked the time: three thirty-five. Still dressed, she crept again from the trailer, around the back of the warehouse, and took up her former vantage point between the crates. As she resumed her position, a little click sounded from the direction of the dorms, then light footsteps came crunching through the snow. Through a knot-hole she could just see the outline of a male figure clad in raincoat and tuque pass by the crates and kneel in front of the capped pipe extensions. His back was to her. A pencil flashlight went on. She could hear the clink of metal against metal, heard him grunt with effort at the task.

She leaned forward on one knee and craned her neck to see. A piece of board, buried in the snow beneath, broke with a crack. The figure glanced quickly around, then stood. The tuque was now visible as a skier's woollen hat with mask. Instinctively she sank back. A great pounding rocked her chest, her breath deepened and the primeval trapped animal within awaited confrontation.

Her mind raced. From her kneeling position she had not been able to judge his height, only that he was tallish and slight. Perhaps she could hold her own long enough for the pipefitter to hear a skirmish, or a scream. Then she realized that it was not she who was trapped but he. She burst forward out of her hiding place in the direction of the warehouse door, bent on rousing the pipefitter to take chase. But her boots had warmed and compressed the snow and as she surged forward she slipped. The mask in the raincoat looked squarely at her, motionless with indecision, then bolted like a frightened deer, along beside the warehouse and around the back of it toward the dorms. Nell raced after him, aware as she did so of the sound of a diesel. The tanker's lights swept over the compound as Nell rounded the corner of the warehouse, just catching the pipefitter's hail of greeting to the trucker.

She reached the far end of the back of the building and came to a stop. Her quarry was no longer in sight. She scanned the distant fenced compound for any sign of motion; all was still. Between the back of the warehouse and the dorms lay a few bushes amidst rock outcroppings, but the light was faint on the snow. Beyond and to the left of the dorms stood larger evergreen trees. Nell's eyes adjusted to the dim light and then she saw the path through the snow towards those trees. It was madness to follow. This man had risked many lives by pulling the ventilation

141

switch; a single life would mean nothing.

She shrugged her shoulders and wandered back to her own trailer, B, in an obvious manner, as though she had given up. She went into her room, turned the light on, left it on for a few moments, then extinguished it. She now crept for a third time to the back door of the trailer, and crouched in front of the darkened window to watch the trees.

A long time passed. Her legs ached with cramp. Should she return to the warehouse and get the pipefitter to go out and beat the bushes for whichever it was? Surely it was either Robin or Dr. Oliver, the only two men who had gone skiing. Both lived in moderate climates and would own raincoats. Should she rouse the camp in this way, and if the search failed, cast aspersions over the whole group and the project as well? She still could not do that. Siegel wanted to play it cool. It was back to square one, as Robin would say, and now even he was under immediate and terrible suspicion.

As she sat at the window thus perplexed, the masked figure emerged from the trees, and with speed and stealth slipped into trailer D.

Nell, numb with disappointment, confusion and cold, returned to her room. Wheels within wheels within wheels. But why Robin? All her instincts cried out against the evidence, but there it was. She wanted to run to his trailer, pound on the door and confront him, but if he were the madman this would be far too dangerous. So she would lock her door and sleep on it, await the solution the morning perspective would bring. Sleep was distant and very slow to come.

♦

The November dawn shone through the curtains onto her face. She awakened with a dead weight of weariness upon her and another weight, too, the weight of loss. Robin, her ally. Robin, who had shared the cardinal. She wanted to cry.

Sunday morning, and no sound but the drone. There were two things she must do. She dressed, put the cellular phone in her purse, and went out the back of the trailer, as if for a walk among the trees. It promised to be a fine morning, clear with little grey

142

clouds. She wandered in the direction of the place he had sprinted from just hours ago but there was not a track to be found; all traces had been brushed clean with an evergreen bough. She followed the swept trail right around the back of the warehouse to its origins at the pipes, said good morning to the trucker, glanced at the caps, and from there strolled over to the parking lot and out along the road.

How clever he was! *How evil.* His duplicity was outrageous. But what on earth could be his motive? He had seemed so wise, so far-seeing, so attuned to the psyche of man. So supportive of Hawthorpe, so forgiving. Why would he want to kill the project? His reasons would be considered, she knew, value-driven.

She had brought the telephone out into the winter landscape to talk to Siegel, tell him the miserable truth, ask him to send an arresting officer. She now found that she must talk to Robin instead, ask for his own accounting. Tell him that if he would not call Siegel himself she had no choice but to report him. This much resolved, she turned back to the project.

Too early on a Sunday morning to take action yet, she thought, passing her own car on the way back. The Siddhu talk did not begin until 11:00 -- people would be sleeping in. There was time to go for a spin, feel things out. The situation just would not compute.

She found herself driving towards the comfortable old brownstone that had sat empty now for nearly a week. Entering, she turned up the heat and made coffee and toast. There, sitting curled up on the chesterfield, a centering of her spirit began to take place.

She put down the coffee and closed her eyes, inviting the quiet, the silence of the empty mind. Counting to four, again and again in a slow unhurried rhythm, her breathing slowed and deepened and the pressure behind her eyes dissolved into a peaceful soft blackness as time melted away.

Presently the body, remote to her now, heaved a large and settled sigh. Her eyes opened. She lay back, all tension gone. A new place, a freedom from concern, the ground of her being, a place from which to act.

Betty Sable drifted into mind, accompanied by a curious feeling of hope and lightness. She remembered that Betty rose at dawn so found the number and dialled.

"Good morning, this is Betty," came the warm and cheerful voice.

"Hi, Betty. It's Nell O'Donovan. Remember me? We flew together..."

"Of *course* I remember you, my dear! I so enjoyed our time together. To what do I owe this pleasure?"

The floodgates opened then and the story poured out. All restraint evaporated in the flow of events, as with keen articulation and sparing no detail she painted the picture to this kindly and receptive mind. It ended with the miserable and inescapable fact of Robin as perpetrator.

"My dear," said Betty with slow deliberation. "Do you *believe* that?"

"No! I *can't* believe it."

"Trust that," said Betty. "Put away your doubts about him and work out what really happened. Go with what you know deep down."

"But the evidence..."

"...is circumstantial. Did you see him remove the mask? No. You are preoccupied with the *fear* that he did it, and that is connected to your feeling for him. Forget all that for the moment. Find out what really happened. *Focus!*"

"I have been! It's been driving me crazy, day and night. I'm too close to it, up to my ears in it..."

"You're overlooking something," said Betty. "There's something you've missed. Listen to your depths and you will see. The knowledge is enfolded within you."

Nell paused. This was getting unreal, but it struck a small chord. "Inner and outer reality?" she asked.

"Yes. You can plumb for truth either way. You have probably witnessed enough already to glean the truth by going in. Like the traditional Naskapi Indians of Labrador. They trusted the Great Man within. They relied upon unconscious revelations to find their way -- both in inner life, and outside, in nature."

"Robin would find this very interesting," thought Nell aloud. "It just can't be him!"

"Of course not! Do me a favour, please. Call me when you find out?"

"If and when," said Nell.

"When," said Betty, laughing. "'Bye for now."

CHAPTER 18

Nell lay back again and closed her eyes, inviting her unconscious to speak. "What am I blocking?" she asked it. "What have I seen that I will not allow?"

An echo tugged at her mind. She took a deep breath and waited. The noise she had heard in the night, the one that had awakened her. It came back. It was a muffled bang on the wall that separated her room from the next. Whose room was it? She had never seen anyone going in or out, nor heard much of anything through the wall. Making a mental note to check the guest list in the office, she stood up, preparing to leave, then paused and went to the telephone.

"Hello, Biz? It's Nell Fitzgerald. Did I wake you?"

"Hi Nell! Don't worry, I'm awake. What's up?"

"I need to ask you something, in confidence. I'll explain later."

"Ask away."

"When you were skiing yesterday, was anyone wearing one of those protective face masks? You know, those wool hats that you pull on?"

"Yes, it was really quite cold. I wished I'd brought mine. Moira had one, so did Robin."

Nell's heart sank. "Thanks Biz," she said dully. "See you later. You coming to hear Siddhu?"

"I'm thinking about it. Are you okay?"

"Fair to middling," said Nell.

"Nell..?"

"I can't talk right now, Biz."

"You're involved in something, aren't you? You're more than a secretary."

"I'll explain later," repeated Nell, her voice hollow. "I've got some figuring to do."

♦

The mood was relaxed, leisurely, low-key. Mintz and Hoff came wandering in with coffee, taking two of the seats that Nell had been setting up for the morning meeting. Hawthorpe appeared in a sweatshirt, actually glowing a little, followed by Miles Oliver, beaming good mornings to everyone through a healthy sunburn.

Once again, the nightmare receded. The team, their work done, was in high spirits; all that remained was the excitement of awaiting the counts.

Hilaire preceded Morgan into the lounge. As they stood together a moment considering where to sit, their hips and thighs just touching, Nell could see the tangible, all but unendurable, excitement between them. They seemed delicately poised on the brink of an abyss.

To Nell's surprise, Cam MacAllister showed up, a little low, she heard him say, because his wife had slipped back again, but he wanted to hear this man a second time.

Zack and Moira arrived together, talking Internet, and Hawthorpe waved them over to the seats beside him. Sam Carney, preoccupied, joined Cam, and the two men shook hands. Kelly and Biz, friends and confidantes, came sailing in and beelined for Nell, who had taken up a vantage point at the back. It was obvious that Biz had repeated Nell's question -- strictly in confidence, of course.

Then Robin appeared, ushering Siddhu through the door ahead of him. Nell could not look at Robin. She busied herself chatting with Biz and Kelly. Light as a feather she strove to be, though someone in this room -- probably Robin -- had seen her last night, falling clumsily between the photomultiplier crates.

Biz looked up and motioned Alex to join them. Jack Suhara walked by, ignoring Nell's little group, and sat by Moira. Siddhu

147

took his former place on the little raised platform, and Robin sat in the front row, occasionally turning to try to catch Nell's wilfully blind eye.

To Nell's relief Siddhu started promptly at eleven.

"Good morning. It is a pleasure to be back in this company. Last week, we were talking about knowledge as symbol for reality, as old truth. If you all agree, we shall continue with that."

There was no dissenting voice.

"All right, then. When I speak of "I", or "me", I am referring to an ongoing, conscious centre of awareness which guides me through life like a pilot or helmsman. This "I" sees, feels, thinks, remembers, chooses, plans, plays, and so on. The psychologists would call this "I" the ego -- the conscious, rational self.

"This ego of mine likes order and control and predictability. In looking out at life, it seeks to impose a cause and effect framework upon the world. We find disorder most stressful, most unacceptable. One vision of hell – John Milton's, in *Paradise Lost* -- had earth, air, fire, and water all topsy-turvy, so that nothing is dependable, nothing can be traversed.

"To the question we are raising, then. Is this cause and effect interface we have with the world, is this ego consciousness with "I" at the centre, is this helmsman or pilot that we call "I"...is this the *only* focus for our experience? And if there is another focus for experience, which does not include "I", does that experience feel separate from reality or is there only the experience of reality itself?"

Again, Nell felt that thunderbolt of otherness, that disembodied oceanic vastness. It's strangeness and unfamiliarity produced a fleeting wave of tension in her solar plexus, driving the vastness away and prodding the ego to stand up like a guard in the night.

Siddhu continued. "Is it possible to step back from the conscious centre and watch its motions? What happens if you separate your attention from the stream of "I" experiences? What happens if this separated awareness simply watches the experiences that arise within consciousness?

"Please do try this and see what happens. The watcher, the observer of the pilot, is separate and above the level of the pilot...so what happens when the observer behind "I" is watching?"

Siddhu paused. Nell looked at the light fixture overhead, and then looked at the looking of it. Her perception altered. A kind of magnified suchness, a sort of jump in dimensionality refocused her awareness of it. It was extraordinary. She looked back at Siddhu, and found his gaze fixed intently upon her.

He resumed. "Consciousness beyond the ego, beyond the known and familiar order -- this is what we wish to explore together. Is there another source of seeing, newly and freshly and fully, the things which is given to our senses?

Nell suddenly realized the profundity of his words. The ego had a way of superimposing old order onto every field of vision. It simply framed a picture it had seen before; it did not see anew. The other centre, behind the ego, co-existed in full dimensionality with the seen. Astounding, remarkable.

"Now may I ask, please, from which centre do you see your physics?" He paused. "Are you lost in your search, carefree, open to the receptive genius within? Or do you already *know* what is real and true, and no longer see freshly? If you know already, does that give you authority to teach others what is fixed and frozen in your mind? Authority to stunt, from your fortress of order and control, the inquiry of fresh minds?"

Nell's attention drifted to Miles Oliver. His physical bearing was tense; anger gripped his hands and shoulders. Lips pursed, the glint of fury was in his eyes. Suddenly she knew -- knew beyond any doubt -- that it was Miles Oliver.

She looked back upon the night before. Through her inner eye she saw him run. It was not Robin. She had seen Robin's easy open grace from behind the day they ran together. The man last night ran with a stealth, with a touch of the theatrical, with a sense of himself as cloak and dagger.

Slipping from her chair, she melted from the room, barely seen. She raced downstairs to her office, pulled out the guest accommodation list. Trailer B. There it was: Dr. Miles Oliver, in the room next to hers. She grabbed the room-keys and her coat and flung out the door and across the compound to the trailer, fitted the key to his lock and entered, going directly to the clothes cupboard. No raincoat. Quickly she rummaged through the drawers. Sweaters, ties, underwear, socks. She unzipped the suitcases. No face mask.

Frantically she looked around, eyed the tables, entered the bathroom. Only the razor kit, neatly arranged, and a dressing gown on the back of the door. Coming out, she glanced through the window. *There he was,* striding purposefully across the compound, close to a run. She looked at the wall that separated their beds, remembered the bang in the night. Dashing across the room, she lifted the corner of the mattress, the bed banged the wall slightly, and ho! they were there, raincoat and mask, folded neatly beneath.

The screen door wrenched open. Desperately she scanned the room for a hiding place; only the bed provided cover. As she reached for the cupboard door, Biz' urgent voice rang out across the compound. "Dr. Oliver! Dr. Oliver! Telephone from London!"

His curse echoed along the corridor with a chilling harshness. The door snapped shut and he retraced his steps to the administration building. Nell straightened the blankets, rezipped the suitcases, locked up, and exited the rear of the trailer to circle around behind the warehouse and re-enter the administration building through the cafeteria.

Returning to the lecture room, she smiled apologetically at Siddhu, covering a yawn by way of explanation and then motioning to her coffee.

Biz leaned over and whispered behind her hand. "The call got cut off."

Outside, beyond the unfolding of Siddhu Krishna's discourse, the tankers droned on. The pipefitter, having slept fairly well, and with his job nearly done, was in good humour. Looking forward to lunch, he barely noticed the second trip Dr. Oliver made to his trailer late that Sunday morning, nor his return through the compound, briefcase in hand, to the parking lot.

Nell longed for the lecture to finish. Longed to explain to Robin, to meet his eye and hold it, to erase her earlier coolness. To share the terrible and unexpected truth about Miles Oliver, and to find a way to apprehend him.

Two things were now clear. Nell knew it was Miles, and he

knew that she knew. Over top of that, he was wily, quick-thinking and dangerous. He had shown foresight in not wearing the mask skiing the day before, cold as it had been. He must have planned to change the caps even before the ski outing. Observed in the act of changing the caps, it had been sheer brilliance to return to Robin's trailer, and later to erase the prints. Showing up at the lecture was incredible -- brazen -- in his knowledge that a young woman had been his witness, yet failing to attend would have been worse. His living mask -- his face -- was perfect, his confidence sublime.

Over the drone of the pumpers, she heard the engine start. She knew that at this very moment he was taking the evidence to town to dispose of it before lunch. Had he bought the interrupted telephone call story? If not, Biz was in danger too.

Nell and Robin would check the mattress and the evidence would be gone. It would be her word against his, the renowned Dr. Oliver, about to be knighted. Surely after fifty years something in his past must tell against him. There must be secrets for such a man as he.

Her attention returned to the room. Siddhu's fine long fingers held up his pocket watch. "I see that it is noon. Is an hour enough for today? You must be ready for lunch." With that he stood and stepped down from the platform. Fortunately, Cam MacAllister arose and approached Siddhu with a question. This gave Nell the opening she needed with Robin.

"I must see you immediately," she said. "It's terribly urgent. Can you get away?"

Robin looked surprised. "I was going to have lunch with Siddhu, here in the cafeteria. I'll ask Cam to take him over instead. I'll join them later."

"Come to my trailer," she said, buttoning her coat.

No sooner had she shut the door than he knocked. "What on earth?" he asked.

"Robin, come with me," and she unlocked Miles' door and went straight to the mattress and lifted it. There was nothing to show for it, not an impression in the sheet, not a thread, nothing.

"Gone! Just as I thought!" she said. "Twenty minutes ago I saw the evidence that would convict Miles Oliver of sabotage."

"Under his mattress? What evidence?"

Nell quickly reiterated the nocturnal cat and mouse game that had unfolded while Robin slept, omitting her suspicion that the masked figure had been Robin himself.

"Nell, you're crazy! You could have been killed! God, woman, I told you that if there was any trouble at all to come and get me!"

"There wasn't time! I was right in the middle of it before I knew what was happening! And when he finally did emerge from the trees he went straight into trailer D..."

"...so you thought it could've been me, eh?" One eyebrow arched up in his sideways glance.

Don't spoil things, she thought. Tread carefully. "Robin, deep down I knew it couldn't be you. But I had to keep an open mind -- I had to deal with the *facts.* That meant allowing for the possibility that I could have been wrong about you." It sounded weak, lame. She looked at the floor, felt the colour rising in her face.

"Just teasing," he said lightly. "You couldn't have gone into trailer D anyway."

"No, I couldn't very well, could I?" She flicked a glance at him. He was grinning broadly. The devil. "Well," she said, "I guess I'll call Mr. Siegel and see what he wants to do about it."

"There's still no evidence," said Robin. "He'll probably want to call London, check him out."

"Robin, you should have seen his face in the lecture today -- a kind of malignant fury. That's when I knew for sure. I left to look for the mask."

"And he followed you. You do take chances, Nell. What time's the underground tour this afternoon?"

"Two o'clock. He's going to strike again...I can feel it."

Robin looked at his watch. "It's 12:15 now. I suggest you call Siegel from my room, then join us for lunch in the cafeteria. It'll take him a while to check Miles out and get back to us. If I see Miles drive into the lot I'll come to warn you. Here's the key."

"It's okay, I have the room keys here. Don't bother warning me. I'd rather wait in your room for the call and keep an eye out -- see what he does when he gets back."

"If you must, but *stay* there! Lock the door. I'll cut lunch short and bring you a sandwich. We'll work out a way to keep

152

him under observation when we go below this afternoon."

As they rose from Miles Oliver's bed where they had been sitting, Nell glimpsed a scratch pad on the bedside table. The page held no writing, but at an angle to the light the imprint of a telephone number could just be made out. She copied it for Siegel.

CHAPTER 19

Nell sat at the window and waited. Time hung motionless. The hands of her watch seemed frozen to the dial.

Though Siegel had good contacts, it was late Sunday afternoon in London, and he had been doubtful about getting through.

She paced. The phone lay there, lifeless as a stone. She checked the dialtone...probably in that instant the telephone was ringing busy in Siegel's ear. She cursed her stupidity.

A little pile of books lay upon Robin's dresser, the uppermost a thin, hardbacked volume with a turquoise cover. On the cover was printed in gold, *As a Man Thinketh*. Absently, restless to pass the time, she picked it up.

The book opened to a single stanza in quotation marks.

"Mind is the Master power that moulds and makes,
And Man is Mind, and evermore he takes
The tool of Thought, and, shaping what he wills,
Brings forth a thousand joys, a thousand ills:--
He thinks in secret, and it comes to pass:
Environment is but his looking-glass."

The hair on her forearms lifted slightly. What was it? Not a chill, surely. No, it was a glimpse of the ineffable. Who had written it?

Something on this trip, this project, was driving Nell into her depths. Uncanny, the synchronicity between the cosmic probe of outer space, and the inner vastness of consciousness. And what Mind contained the Mind of Man?

The cell phone warbled, jarring her out of the thoughts.

"Where are you?" His voice was urgent.

"In Robin's room. The door's locked."

"Could anyone listen in?"

"I'd hear the click."

"Good. We're in luck. I know a chap over there, Jeremy Falwell. He uncovered a great deal in a short time. Our friend has a secret life."

"It had to be."

"My contact has access to police records. About three years ago, our man was discovered in an uptown London brothel during a discreet raid. The point of the raid was AIDS control -- condoms -- not to harass the girls. But it was bad timing for Miles. He was found coupled with a Pakistani boy. They booked him."

"That explains something I saw!" said Nell. "He was furious at the Indonesian lad who interrupted his lecture. Later, down in the mine, he was just the opposite with the boy -- *tender!* It was odd."

"Still at it, then," said Siegel with disgust. "Well, because of his connections, and his publishing, they hushed it up. But there was a condition. He was made to see a psychiatrist."

"Did you talk to the psychiatrist?" asked Nell in disbelief.

"Not me. Impossible. Patient confidentiality," replied Siegel. "But my contact knows a doctor who called the psychiatrist and got an off-the-record opinion. We are dealing with a disturbed man. Cornered, he could be extremely dangerous."

"What's the matter with him?"

"Something about narcissism, he said. "Driven by power needs. He grew up in a good family, but poor -- an only child. Father killed in the war. An uncle helped the family and sent him away to school. He was small for his age, picked on by bullies. So he withdrew -- retreated into studies. He became something of a prodigy, top boy in his form. When he finally started to grow he was handsome to boot."

"What went wrong?" she asked.

"Split-off something or other, the doctor said. The gist being, that to escape the vulnerable boy inside, he tailored himself into a kind of paragon of knowledge and power. That telephone number you gave me is in the Secretary of State Department. He's been nominated for a knighthood for his contribution to education, but if this project refutes the solar model his books will be obsolete. And a new CD-ROM he's got in the works will be out the window as well."

"So Robin was right, then, bringing in Siddhu and Hernandez. Whenever anyone points to a new physics, he strikes at the project. His face was *terrible* this morning! He's in a corner, all right."

"Yes. Now listen, Nell. You keep away from Miles Oliver. You're his only witness. He's going to try to arrange an accident for the project that will finish you off as well. He's ripe, he's primed. He'll try this afternoon, down there with the group. I'm ordering you to stay up top. Got that?"

Nell was reluctant. "If you say so."

"I *do* say so. And there's something else. He's fit. He mountaineers. He did Everest a couple of years ago."

"He's over fifty!"

"Never mind, he's strong as an ox. Now get Robin to phone me, a.s.a.p. I'll call Bridges and alert him that we'll be keeping Oliver under surveillance. If he's as desperate as we think he is, he'll strike whether it's safe or not. Then we'll have him, poor bastard."

The key sounded in the lock. "Robin's here now."

"Good. Wait! Second thoughts. I want you to leave the project, just get out of there. Get in your car now and go to the apartment. We'll call you in an hour or so."

Nell felt a surge of disappointment. How could he take her off the job at the crucial moment? "It's not *over* yet!" she protested.

"This is not a movie, Mrs. O'Donovan. It's real life and you are in imminent danger. You've done a wonderful job for us. We have our man hooked now -- it's just a matter of netting him. Please, do as I ask! Put Robin on now."

Nell handed the phone over and a moment later he looked at her, nodding his head, saying, "Yes, I'll make sure she does." After a long series of yes's, Robin bid Siegel goodbye and folded the telephone shut.

156

"Things are moving fast," said Robin. "I've got to call the piepfitter, tell him to watch Oliver like a hawk. It's 1:40 now. I'm to come with you while you pack, and see you out to your car. We've just got time before the trip down to the observatory."

"Robin! What if I pass him on the road out there? He's not back yet!"

"You're right, we didn't think of that. Okay. We'll load your car. Then, if he's not back, we'll wait in the cafeteria until he shows up."

As arranged, the group of engineers, physicists, and systems people began to congregate in the cafeteria just before two. Miles had still not returned. Nell and Robin were sitting at separate tables, she reading by the exit to the parking lot, he chatting with Siddhu.

At two o'clock, Bridges came in and did a head-count. Too many for the changerooms, he said. They'd do two trips. He was just asking for volunteers for the first trip down when Miles Oliver pulled up outside, and came blustering in with a huge Black Forest cake he'd picked up at a local restaurant. He placed it on Nell's table, then beamed at the group. "For later," he said, rubbing his hands together, "to celebrate!"

It was so brilliant Nell began to doubt her own sanity. How could this man be a villain? She glanced at Robin -- his face, too, was incredulous.

"Well done, Miles!" said Bridges heartily, clapping him on the shoulder. Had Siegel not got through to him? "Now, who's for the first trip?"

"The sooner down, the sooner back!" chortled Miles, pointing to the cake and laughing. He'd probably find a way to delay his return, thought Nell, he'd try to take the second elevator back up.

"Right on, Miles!" joined in Robin. "Black Forest's my favourite too!"

Siddhu, Mintz and Hoff, Cam MacAllister, Moira, and Jack Suhara also motioned to go first. Suhara was to drive the tram.

"Okay," said Mike. "You first lot, you'll shower and put on the coveralls, then go to the control room. Jack, while group one is in the control room, you come back and pick up group two. When group two gets to the control room, Jack'll take you first lot

157

down to see the bottom of the cavity, through the bulkhead window. It's illuminated, like an undersea garden. It's terrific! After you've all had a good look, Jack'll drive you back to the lift, then go back for the second group."

Bridges led the way, then Miles. As he left Nell's table, Miles leaned over and looked into her eyes, his own kindly and paternal.

"Why Nell! Are we to miss the pleasure of your company? I was so looking forward to having you along!"

"...to pushing me over the edge!" she thought. Even now, he was irresistibly charming. It was not difficult to fall into her usual role with him. "I'll make sure we overlap," she said warmly, placing a hand on his sleeve. "See you down there!"

Robin passed next, glanced sternly at her, then meaningfully towards the parking lot. She nodded and resumed reading, looking the part. If Miles were going to blow the place to smithereens, at least he'd await her arrival.

Inexplicably, she tarried after Miles was out of sight. A few moments later, Kelly breezed in, cheeks red from her noon outing. "There you are, Nell. Looks like we'll be going down together. Biz and I were late so they split us up -- too many on the first trip."

Nell froze inwardly and swallowed. "Biz has gone down?"

"Yeah. That's fine. She wanted to get some work done today. She'll have more time this way."

Kelly seemed innocent of any knowledge. "Gotta use the washroom," said Nell, excusing herself. God Almighty! Robin didn't know! Didn't know the phone call from London was a hoax. Biz was now in mortal danger.

She entered the Ladies', searching desperately for anything, anything at all. She unscrewed the soap dispenser, took it to the office and taped the open end securely shut. Then her eyes lit on a pair of heavy-duty paper shears. She slipped them into her purse, returned to the cafeteria, and sleight-of-handed a dinner knife in on top of them -- for Biz.

Mike came back for the second crew, helped Nell on with her coat. It was now obvious that he didn't know. Siegel and Robin were going to have a mutual attack of apoplexy. Where in God's name was Biz at this moment? Walking along behind the tram, gaily chatting with the man who needed her dead? God help her, prayed Nell.

Take it easy, she thought, entering the warehouse, Zack holding the door. Don't panic. Miles Oliver is going to wait his chance. He will take me and Biz and the project together, if he can. If Biz falls by the wayside too early she'll be missed. Nell calmed herself, managed to chat a little while the cable squeaked around the drum, hoisting the lift to the surface.

Bridges had remained topside to oversee the filling process. In her group were Hawthorpe, Alex Wong, Kelly, Hilaire and Morgan, Sam Carney, and Zack. For the first time now, in the presence of real and overriding danger, she was not claustrophobic. But she feigned her usual nerves, thrust her hands deep into her pockets and stood rigidly staring at her shoes.

"Focus," as Betty Sable had said. *Focus!*

What can he do with Robin and the pipefitter dogging his steps? He'll need to lose them. To do what? Start a fire? Knock a hole in the acrylic tank? Flood the tunnel from the great bulkhead at the base? One thing was certain: he must wait for her.

Jack Suhara was waiting in the tram for them when the lift doors opened. Nell held back, appearing to search her purse. She lifted the lid of the steel toolbox and grasped the long Magnum flashlight, transferring it to the purse. That was odd -- there had been two before, and a large heavy wrench. This is an emergency kit, she thought. *He's* got them! Politely waited until last, then slipped them like quicksilver into his duffel coat.

She walked, leading the single file of pedestrians along the tunnel behind the tram. Avoiding chatter, she was free to note and memorize the side-drifts off the main tunnel. She strode along, each step a yard, pacing the distances. Having formed a mental map, she reversed it in readiness for the trip back. But what good would her map be beyond those dark tunnel openings? Who knew what depths and recesses lay within?

The men and women parted company at the changerooms. Hilaire and Kelly showered first, then dressed while Nell showered.

"Go ahead, guys. I'll catch you up." She fit the flashlight and the bottle of soap under her belt, then stepped into coveralls and sank the knife and shears deep into the pockets. Lacing the runners snugly, she was grounded and ready for action.

In that moment of readiness, inspiration struck. He would

hide. He would melt into a corner and lose himself. But where? Oh God, he had the code -- he'd casually asked Biz for it the day he drove the tram. The doors would present no obstacle, then. He could afford to leave the observatory with the others and return to it later.

He would wait until the tram was taking him back, then duck into one of those tunnels. There he would be at large, as hard to track as a thief in a black forest. *The cake!* Was he amusing himself, leaving clues in a cat and mouse game, laughing at their stupidity? *Unspeakable arrogance!*

Nell ran along the pristine corridor to the igloo-entrance of the control room. Stopping in front of the flanged doors, she peered through its little window. The first person she saw was Robin, standing beside the pipefitter, talking in a low voice. Hilaire, Zack, and Hawthorpe were listening to Kelly. Robin and the pipefitter had joined the second group! Then she understood why.

Miles Oliver was there too -- he'd hung back as she had expected. He was seated at one of the computers, examining a "you-are-here" map of the observatory and the mine beyond. She'd remembered seeing him looking at it the day of the student tour as well. He's going to jump the trolley and hit one of those tunnels, she thought. He's got a flashlight and a heavy wrench. The first group will have gone up and there'll be just Biz working here when he comes back. Not if I can damn-well help it!

She had to make the expected appearance. Taking a deep breath, she pushed through the swinging door, smiling brightly. Robin looked as if he'd seen a ghost. Nell went straight to Miles, peered over his shoulder at the honeycomb of tunnels, and spoke.

"So Dr. Oliver, we *have* caught up with you! I *thought* the two groups might overlap!"

"Hullo m'dear," said Miles easily. "Fascinating, this mine! Can you imagine the mining chaps down here, keeping their bearings in this maze of rock?"

"I'm sure their wives were worried sick," she replied, mentally snapshotting the drifts off the main tunnel outside the project. Her eye was drawn to an abandonned shaft marked "Danger!"

Sam Carney spoke. "Well folks, we'd better move on. Don't wanna keep Jack waiting."

"Oh!" said Nell in disappointment. "I've only just arrived!

Perhaps I'll stay with Biz and see the undersea gardens later."

Robin smiled faintly at her, relieved but puzzled. Lagging behind as group two filed by, he leaned towards her, his face a living question mark.

She whispered quickly, "He needs to get Biz!"

"You two stay put!" ordered Robin. "I'll come back for you after we get him up top." Miles had wandered out to the deck. The pipefitter drifted over to the door to watch him.

"He hasn't tried anything," said Robin. "Not a shred of evidence."

"We've got to give him a chance...set him up," she replied. "I think he'll make a break for it in the tunnel on the way out, then come back here to arrange an accident."

"He won't be able to get past those doors..."

"He's got the *code!* He used it to drive the tram last week!"

"God, he thinks of everything!" said Robin. "If he makes a break for it we'll be right behind him."

"Don't let him out of your sight," she warned. "He's incredibly quick, and he's got a wrench!"

Miles returned from the deck, shaking his head in amazement. "Jolly fine job of it!" and he followed the others out of the lab, Robin and the pipefitter on his tail.

Nell ran over to Biz. "Biz! You're in terrible danger! You saved me in the trailer and he must suspect! It's been Miles all along -- how did you know?"

"Instinct," said Biz. "The way he looked this morning."

"I'm going to play a hunch," said Nell. "No time to explain. If he gets by us and comes back he'll try to kill you. He's got the door code."

"Fool, me! I gave it to him! Too late to change it now." Biz bit her lip, thinking. "I'm a sitting duck, eh? Well, ducks can swim, can't they? If he comes back I'll go over the side!"

"You won't hear him," Nell cautioned.

"Ah, but I will! There's a buzzer and a remote camera at the door. They're usually off. I'll activate them."

"Brilliant! Here, for what it's worth," and she handed Biz the knife. "What's that code again?"

"37741K."

"Be careful Biz. He's mad."

"Nell...don't take any chances! Who *are* you, anyway?"

"A sleuth of sorts," and she darted out the flanged door and along the corridor to the tunnel.

CHAPTER 20

There was no time to lose. She punched the code into the panel and the door rolled up, then down again, and she was outside in the timeless underground silence, carved out and thinly lit by man. The new Adidas sped her along the glinting tracks to the main tunnel, where she rounded the corner to the right and soon came upon the first of the drift tunnels off the main route.

She stopped. There was not a sound. Had the second group passed by already on the return trip? No! Not a whiff of diesel...not enough time. Unsure, she walked on. Her mental map showed a larger tunnel, off to the right, around a bend in the main line. There, there it was. On the computer map it had shown as "The Honeycomb". That's where I'd go, she thought, wait it out in my memorized maze and then return to the lab to set up the unfortunate accident. And where had I disappeared to? I'd always wanted to explore that honeycomb -- got lost trying.

Nell reached for the Magnum and crept into the musty darkness. Almost immediately she was confronted with a side tunnel that ran off to the left in the direction of the lift. A hiding place, and, further along, another. Leaving the first spot for Miles, she made her way to the second, stood inside it and extiguished the light.

Group two stood in line in front of the thick window at the base of the cavity and took turns peering into the illuminated watery vastness. Mirrors inside the heavy bulkhead doors revealed the underside enormity of the great soccer ball, stabilized by ropes as it floated peacefully in its tranquil ultrapure medium.

Jack Suhara waited patiently while the physicists drank in the spectacle of the completed project. Then, one by one, the group remounted the tram, Sam Carney in the passenger seat, and Robin sitting next to Miles in the back seat, behind Jack.

The strong young pipefitter walked behind the tram, his attention on Miles Oliver. The people on foot behind him were losing a little ground on the uphill journey behind the tram.

The tram drew up to the junction at the end of the project's norite drift, slowed for the turn into the main tunnel, and was picking up speed as it rounded a bend. At that moment Miles Oliver vaulted from his seat in the tram, and in one deft perfectly-timed movement, tucked his head and somersaulted his arched body into the blackness of the drift. The tram was already past the entrance by the time Robin had thrust himself from his own door and lept the tracks in pursuit. No sooner had he entered the tunnel than he felt a cracking blow to the back of his head, and blackness engulfed him as he sagged to the ground.

The pipefitter, rounding the bend in the tracks on foot, was dismayed to see the tram ten paces ahead of him with only two occupants. Reaching for his flashlight he raced for the tunnel, yelling to those behind him to follow the tram. Switching on the powerful beam, he rocketed into the tunnel, then, realizing his folly, he switched it off, listening. A second dull thud resounded in the drift, and Miles Oliver heaved the large body into the side drift beside Robin's. "Fools!" he muttered aloud. "Damn meddling fools."

Nell stood hidden in the entrance to the second drift and waited in the shadows. It seemed an eternity. Then she heard it, the far-off ticking of the diesel. It's small vibration echoed underfoot. Louder and louder it grew, until the passing vehicle darkened the entrance to the drift. A figure spun through the air to land like a cat and came up smoothly to its feet, then ducked into the first drift on her side of the tunnel.

Another figure plunged in behind the first. In dim silhouette against the main tunnel light she saw the arm and the wrench descend, hit home, and the figure collapsed without a sound. As she stood in stunned silence, a flashlight beam bounced over the dull black rock and then clicked off. The arm and wrench came down with a vengeance, a truncated oath rang out, and the young hulk's knees folded. An English voice, ugly with scorn and contempt, spat "Fools!" as its owner raced from the drift, turning back towards the project.

Nell rushed to Robin. He lay there, face down, arms outstretched, out cold, breathing. Blood matted the hair behind his left ear -- it had been a glancing blow.

She flicked the beam to the pipefitter and knew at once with a final and sickening certainty that the crumpled mass of muscle and bone would never breathe again. All vitality drained in an instant, a lifetime of vigor crushed with contempt.

Nell was gripped by a cold fury, a steel resolve to bring the fiend to bay. In a heightened, altered state she took to her heels in chase, flying headlong back down the main tunnel to the lab. Reaching the door, hand poised to enter the code, she glanced up, saw the little camera eye and recoiled, shrinking to the side. Where was he now?

Her mind raced. The buzzer had sounded, Biz had seen him on the screen and climbed over the edge, into the ultrapure. Had he noticed the warning system, guessing they'd seen him? Or had he rushed in blindly to search them out and snuff them?

She stood very still, cupping her ear, listening. Not the tiniest hum. Reaching up, she held a hand to the side of the camera. No vibration. She stood on tiptoes, craning her head. There was a pinpoint of red plastic on the far side at the back, not illuminated: it was off! No buzzer would sound. Bless you, Biz, you think of everything!

Nell entered, tore past the car-wash, the change rooms, down the neon whiteness to the igloo entrance. She froze. The lights were out, the laboratory in darkness. Had Biz shut everything down as if they'd gone for the day, then slipped over the edge to hide?

A bruising hand clamped tight against her mouth and her left arm was wrenched cruelly up between her shoulder blades. He worked the wadded handkerchief into her mouth and propelled her forcibly through the flanged doors, snapped on the lights, and swept her across the expanse of floor to the computers. With his free hand and his teeth he tore off a length of plastic tape and stretched it with suffocating pressure across her mouth and around her head. He thrust her into a chair, ripping off more tape. When she kicked out at him he slapped her hard across the side of the head; the chair reeled. Steadying it, he swung it around on its casters, knelt on the floor and swiftly taped her wrists and ankles behind. The whole process took less than thirty seconds.

"Now, my dear Ms. Fitgzerald, we'll see how smart you are...where is Biz Castle?"

Nell shrugged hopelessly. With the back of his hand he dealt a savage blow to her right cheek. Nausea swelled like a wave inside her. Swallowing hard, she willed herself not to retch and choke. Teeth set against the shock she held her eyes to the floor. Through the haze of pain came the image of a grizzly -- to look him in the eye drives him mad with rage.

"There's only one place she can be," he seethed, "and that's taking a swim in the ultrapure." He gave the chair a wild push in the direction of the deck. It careened through the swinging doors and crashed into the rail beyond. Racing out he snatched up the chair and balanced her on the rail, barking hoarsely into her ear. "Is she down there? She'll never help you now...you'll sink like a stone!"

At that moment Biz' head appeared, soaking wet, at the top of a nearby ladder. "Please, sir! Please! Put her down. Let's talk. It's not too late!"

Nell's heart sank. It was far too late. If only the pipefitter had left his flashlight off, he wouldn't have been such a target. But wait...Miles still had a chance to pull it off. With the women taken care of in the accident, Robin and the pipefitter could meet their end in the abandoned shaft she'd seen on the map. If that was his plan he'd have to move fast, as Suhara and Bridges would be back with the police. A tragic and disoriented Dr. Oliver would emerge from the maze, anguished and guilt-ridden over the two men, himself the lone survivor.

"There's no time for talk," said Miles matter-of-factly. "That pipefitter's dead, poor lad. His skull split like an eggshell. You!" he cried, pointing at Biz. "Wheel this slut out of here and down the ramp."

Biz hesitated. Furious, he whipped out the wrench and raised it over Nell's head. "Move!"

Biz obediently pushed Nell, wheelchair-style, back into the control room, through the corridors, out into the tunnel and down the ramp to the door at the bottom.

"The parting of the ways," he said. He entered the code and the door rolled up into its ceiling slot. "Get her into the tunnel and pull that tape off her, *fast!*" Biz tore off the tape lest he smack Nell with the wrench. He grabbed the chair and backed out the door with it, entered the code and the door rolled shut.

Inside, Biz and Nell could hear the clunk of the mechanical lever as he locked the door in place.

"He's going to open the bulkhead doors," said Nell simply. "We're supposed to drown."

"How do you know?" asked Biz, alarmed.

"It'll look like an accident. You and I stayed behind, remember? To come down here later and look through the glass. Something went wrong with the hydraulics and the bulkhead opened. That's why he took the chair away -- it would have been evidence."

Biz saw it all then. She shuddered. "We've got about two minutes until he gets back up there."

"Come on!" shouted Nell. They raced down the tracks to the hydraulic doors. There, through the glass, in its remote stillness, hung the huge ball, glittering dimly in the gloom.

"The ultrapure will surge along here like a tidal wave," said Nell. "The ball will smash the side of the cavity and break. We need a handhold! Once the water's risen, we'll have to swim for it, down into the cavity, then up to the surface!"

Desperately they scanned the lower tunnel for something -- anything -- that would secure them. Nothing, except a firehose behind a glass door in the tunnel wall. Above it was a gravity feed tank, a big drum bolted to the rock, with welded handles either end. "Biz! There, quick! I'll give you a leg-up. Grab those handles and when the water rises, hold on for dear life."

Nell, the taller, jumped for the handles at the other end of the drum, and an instant later the bulkhead doors started to inch apart. It began as a thin vertical jet. As the doors wound open it widened to a river, cascading past their feet. Doors fully open now, the raging torrent surged past them, tugging wildly at their lower bodies, swirling their legs downstream. The deluge rose to breast level, then to chin. Nell gave the signal and they filled their as they submerged, praying the air would last until the water found its level in the drift.

Nell's lungs, though bursting, held. Thank God for those early morning runs! Biz, upstream, was losing her grip on the handles. As she drifted by, Nell let go of a handle and grabbed a wrist. In that tumultuous torrent she closed her eyes and riveted all the will in her being into those two clenched hands.

Her grip was failing now, the handle slipping from her grasp. In her mind's eye she saw their bodies, drowned against that bolted door. The headlines loomed -- two young women dead and a multimillion dollar loss.

And then the current slackened, stopped, ebbed back, like water sloshing in a tub. Lungs screaming, they dove through the bulkhead doors, kicked furiously around the shadowy globe above, and broke the surface gasping sweet air.

Treading water in a dream, they looked around the murky dimness of the cavity. Miraculously, the great ball was intact, hanging lopsidedly on its ropes, still partially submerged in the ultrapure.

A moment later the weak light went out completely.

Nell tread water in the inky blackness, the darkest place she had ever been. Equilibrium had returned to the cavity, the water barely lapping against the shotcrete walls.

"Biz?" she whispered. "You okay?"

"Right here," said Biz softly. "He could still be up there."

"He won't stay long," said Nell. "Jack and Mike will be coming back."

"I sure hope so! I know how to get up. There are rungs in the rock leading up to the girders that support the control deck. It'll be a climb, maybe fifty feet. We can manage that, but I don't know how we're going to span that girder in the dark."

Nell suddenly remembered the flashlight. Her coveralls were still on, the flashlight weighing heavily in the deep pocket against her leg.

"Biz, I've got the flashlight! Here, cup your hands around it and we'll try it out."

Hiding the Magnum between them, she switched it on. The strong light showed redly between Biz' folded hands.

"Thank God!" said Nell. "I think there's been a power failure. If he's up there trying to confirm the damage, he'll be using a flashlight. We'll keep this one off and swim to the side and look up."

They struck out in the warm black void of water, swimming a slow crawl, hushed whispers their only contact. Biz, leading the way, ran into something.

"Stop! I've hit the side of the ball. Okay, Nell, if we swim straight back we'll run into the cavity wall. Then we can feel our way around to the rungs."

A few moments later they touched the wall and looked up. No light, not a photon, anywhere in the cavity.

"He can't be there," said Nell. "He's left us for dead. He's gone to take care of Robin."

She switched on the light, desperate to stop him. The beam swept around the cavity perimeter and came to rest on the ascending rungs. Swimming furiously they made for the ladder, Nell ahead. Foot on the rung now, she shone the light straight up, calculating the distance to the I-beam, then replaced the light in her pocket, hand-over-handing up the ink-black wall like a human fly.

Suddenly her right hand grasped empty air, throwing her off balance. "Stop!" she said to Biz. "We're at the top." She turned on the light to find herself perched on a rung beside a heavy beam encased in shotcrete, at hip level. The idea was to get onto it and somehow wriggle across to the ladder that hung down from the control deck.

It was about six feet across. She shone the light downwards. Far below, the beam found its mirror in the ultrapure pool, the rungs on one side and the great soccer ball on the other. Shaken, she switched off the light to steady her nerves.

Funk: the enemy, the undoer, the thief of good intent. She took a deep breath to quell the trembling, told herself it was trembling, simple trembling, nothing more. Why let it slay sweet reason? "Biz, hold the light for me," and she eased her butt onto the girder, raised her leg over it, and leaned forward, reaching down on either side to grasp the underlying edges of the beam.

169

Balanced, she pulled herself along, walking one buttock after the other across the abyss below.

When she reached the deck it was a simple matter to grasp the ladder and climb up and over the railing.

"Well done!" whispered Biz. "There's a flashlight on a bracket just inside the door there."

Nell reached inside, found the bracket. Empty. "Biz, it's gone. You'll have to toss me the light!"

Biz turned the light on, gauged the distance from where she stood on the top rung to Nell's hands behind the railing above -- about twelve feet. She took a couple of practice swings, then tossed the foot-long cylinder in a high, lazy trajectory. It spun slowly, end over end, high up over the rail, falling softly into Nell's outstretched hands.

"Partner in crime!" said Nell with respect. "How cool you are!"

Biz grinned, crawled across the girder, climbed to the deck and entered the control room. She tried the lights: they were dead. The telephone, alive. Biz dialled the warehouse and Bridges grabbed it on the first ring.

"Where are you, Biz?"

"In the control room, with Nell. Miles Oliver tried to sack the project -- opened the hydraulic doors, flooded the drift. The ultrapure's half gone and the ball's hanging by a thread."

"Hold on!" said Bridges. Biz could hear him yelling at them to stop the filling.

"Where's Oliver?" he shouted.

"Talk to Nell," said Biz, passing the 'phone.

"He knocked Robin out and killed the pipefitter," said Nell. "I think he's gone back to the honeycomb to dispose of them. He left Biz and me for dead -- tried to drown us in the lower tunnel."

"Christ almighty! So he's back in the honeycomb! Well I've bad news for you. The cage jammed when the lights went out. Jack and Group Two are stuck in it. Power's out all over the project -- must've shorted in the flood."

Poor Hawthorpe, stuck in the elevator. "Mike -- that honeycomb. He memorized it. There's an abandoned shaft in there. Do you know where it is?"

"Yeah, lemme think. Fourth drift to the left, third tunnel to

170

the right. I went in to see it -- it's bottomless. They fenced it off, took up the tracks, years ago."

"Gotta help Robin," said Nell.

Mike paused. "Would you listen if I told you to sit tight?"

"Can't."

"His sigh was resigned. "The lift mechanic's on his way. So is Hydro. You got guts, lady!"

"Getting by so far," and she hung up.

CHAPTER 21

It took Biz and Nell just under two minutes to run, soaking wet, to the junction of the project drift and the main tunnel. They stopped briefly, turned off the flashlight, and listened. All was quiet. They crept softly through the pitch dark, feeling their way around the bend to the honeycomb drift.

Nell suddenly remembered the shears and the soap dispenser that she had stuck in her belt. Pessimistically, she searched the drenched clothes clinging to her. No scissors, no dispenser...but wait! Something bulky hung outside her right knee. The dispenser! It had been trapped in the leg of the slacks, unnoticed until now in the commotion.

Like bear spray, she hoped. The bear theme kept recurring. Something about the fury in his eyes...savage, glazed over with rage, fearless, single-minded.

"Nell?"

"Yes?"

"Listen!"

Nell put her ear up to the drift. Nothing. She waited. Then there was something...very faint. There it was again. An intermittent dull shuffling, the soft sound of something heavy being dragged along the ground.

"He's dragging the pipefitter," said Nell. "He's a big man, too heavy to carry."

Quietly they watched and listened. Then, far along the drift, his torch went on. His back was towards them. The light played forward along the left tunnel wall, seeking an entrance. It went out again. More dragging...light on again...more searching. At length the light disappeared into what was probably the fourth drift to the left.

"Wait here a sec," Nell said. She stepped into the tunnel, groping her way along to the first drift where the two men had been felled with the wrench. Stepping into the drift she kneeled, briefly shining the light. Robin lay there as before, breathing but unconscious. She laid a finger to his jugular: strong, steady, slow.

She returned to Biz. "Robin's out cold, but he's okay. I think we should move him."

"Where to?"

"I'm trying to think...not back into the main tunnel, in case the power comes on. Up into the next drift would be the best. Miles will think he woke up and left."

"Has he got a light?" asked Biz.

"I didn't see one."

"If he wakes up in the dark he won't know where he is. He wouldn't get very far without a light."

"What else can we do?" asked Nell. "Miles will be back in a few minutes to drag him off to the shaft. If we can get Robin into that next drift it will buy us some time. Come on."

They turned Robin over and, needing both hands to shift him, Nell pocketed the light. They grasped him by the ankles and under the arms. A hundred and seventy-five pounds of dead weight -- they couldn't lift him clear of the ground. Stumbling along in the dark, tripping over loose rocks, they managed to half-drag, half-carry him up to the next drift, where Nell had stood when Robin was hit. Now she stopped, breathing heavily, and set her half down.

"Biz, we'll have to lift him clear of the ground here so there won't be any drag marks going into this tunnel."

They rested a moment, then with a whispered "one-two-three" and a heave they got him around the corner and about ten feet into the tunnel. Nell retraced her steps to the corner and listened. Silence.

She returned to Robin and switched on the Magnum. Up ahead, quite close, was an intersection. If they turned right, it would join up with the third drift. "How about one more corner for good measure?" she asked.

"Good idea." It was hot work. Near exhaustion, and sweating into their wet clothes, they got Robin around the next corner and sat down on the tracks.

"Biz, we have the advantage now. When he gets back there and finds Robin gone he's going to have a real problem. Either Robin came to life and is lost around here without a light, or somebody moved him. Right?"

"Right."

"If someone moved him, they'd stay with him 'til he woke up -- so he wouldn't get lost in the dark. Either way, Miles will figure his quarry is awake and conscious, so he'll be ready to strike out and kill."

"He's killed once," agreed Biz.

"So he'll start to search, probably in a grid -- he had a good look at the map."

"If he keeps his cool."

"He's pretty good at that. I have a hunch he'll take a quick look up the main tunnel, then come back to where he hit Robin and start searching outwards. We'll have to stay out of his sight. He'll find Robin within a few minutes, alone and unconscious -- that'll really spook him."

"He might have come to, crawled a bit, and passed out again," suggested Biz.

"Let's arrange him that way," said Nell.

They got him looking as if he'd been feeling his way along the rock face and then passed out again.

"Now the tough part. One of us hides around the corner there, off to the left -- that's the back of drift three -- in case Robin wakes up. The other goes up drift three to the right -- back up to the main honeycomb drift -- and waits around the corner to crack that devil's skull with the Magnum as he trudges by dragging Robin."

"He might try to kill Robin first."

"If he raises that wrench you'll have time to scream and I'll run back and we'll fight him right here."

"It's a bit complicated but it might work," said Biz uncertainly.

"I'd better take another look," said Nell, edging back to the honeycomb's main tunnel. Before she reached it, she could see his light, very near, hear his footfall.

174

She melted back into the drift, felt her way along to Biz. "He's coming now!" she whispered, leading Biz to her spot kitty-corner from Robin and just a few paces away. "You'll be close enough to see Miles clearly from his own light. How're you doing?"

"I may have no light," said Biz, "but I'm fighting mad!"

"Take this," said Nell. "It's soap. If he gets too close, throw it in his eyes. It might slow him down."

They took up their posts.

Nell heard Mike's Auzzie accent. "Robin? Where the hell are ya, mate? Robin? Come on, lad, give us a shout!"

She looked out from her hiding place and saw the flashlight coming up the drift, but the main tunnel beyond was in darkness. The power was still off: it *couldn't* be Mike!

Miles was doing the unexpected, calling his quarry to him.

He was abreast of drift two. "Robin? Robin? It's Bridges...can you hear me, Robin?"

"In here, Mike," came Robin's muffled voice. Nell reacted impulsively. She sprinted back to the second drift, tore in after him, and reached the scene just as Miles was raising the wrench over Robin, who was climbing to his feet, one arm up to ward off the blow.

"Dr. Oliver!" cried Nell, shining the light into her own face. "I am your witness!" In that half light, Oliver's face fell in disbelief. Then fury unleashed itself.

"Bitch!" he screamed with spine-chilling rage, and launched himself at her like a demon from hell.

Nell turned on her heels and ran, ran like the wind, plunging left at drift four, then dove down a tunnel to the right. Flashing the light at intervals, she groped desperately along the dark rock face to steady her steps.

Turn after turn she took, dodging this way, feigning that, in a frenzied quest to disorient him, elude him, and wait for help. But ever quick, he kept pace, his light bobbing doggedly behind, throwing up shadows on the rock ahead.

Nell took a turn to the left, flicked on the light, and her heart stopped. It was a dead end. He was too close. The game was up.

Something in her could not accept it. Light out now, she dropped to her knees, feeling blindly along that tunnel of death for any nook or cranny. His steps echoed in the drift outside, his light flickered from around the corner. Then she felt a little stir of air, a tiny draft. She followed it, crossing the tracks at the end of the tunnel in a low crouch. Her hands splayed imploringly over the rocks, the draft became stronger. She reached the corner, and there it was! A narrow opening. She wriggled into it, hands scraping against the rock, dust clinging to her hair.

No sooner had she got the length of her body into that crawl-space than his flashlight beam scoured the dead-end at her feet. Holding her breath like a hunted animal, she waited on the fates.

In an instant the light was gone. She heard his curse of disgust, his retreating steps. She lay still, breath shallow, owing her maker.

Then, as if in a straight-jacket, she began to elbow her way along, not daring to use the light. Instead, she placed the Magnum ahead of her, worked her way up to it, then moved it again. As she made her way at this snail's pace, the cleft widened a little and the air changed.

Suddenly the overhead rock was gone, and in the same moment the flashlight slipped away from her opening hand, fell a short distance and bounced. As it did so it came on for a second, its arcing beam painting the walls of the shaft. Having performed to perfection its final act, the light disappeared soundlessly from sight. Seconds later, the hollow echo of it striking bottom drifted up to her marvelling ear.

She took stock. She had lost him. He had not seen the crawl-space. There was no light, no sound. Only her own breath, the encasing cleft, the emptiness ahead -- and that unnerving absolute blackness.

Again a headline loomed in her mind, bold and clear in black and white. "Galiano woman found dead in mineshaft."

A chill went through her as she fully grasped the terror of her situation, grasped how utterly and remotely lost she was. Panic was igniting, its deadly ripple tugging at her heart. No! she cried inwardly. Not this! With a shuddering breath she clenched her fists shut, then opened them and placed her hands flat against the ancient rock. It was warm.

"I am lying on solid, warm rock and I can breathe the air." The affirmation steadied her. "I am in no immediate danger.

They will find me." Panic retreated. She smiled a little, surprised and encouraged by her own pluck.

What now? For the moment, it seemed best to stay put, out of sight in case he returned. If a search party came looking for her she would yell out. Going anywhere at all was futile; she'd lost all sense of direction long ago.

Where had he gone, she wondered vaguely. Where was Robin? Biz? Were the lights on yet? It all seemed so far away. Exhausted, the rock almost comfortable beneath her, she dozed.

And then it came. A long, piercing, angry scream, loud and clear and close. A heavy thud echoed softly up from the depths below. Nell knew then that Miles Oliver was dead in the chasm, and felt the weight of his evil spirit lift from the land of the living.

What had happened? Had he stumbled into the shaft, running from his pursuers? Had he jumped deliberately? Had Robin been following them all along?

"Robin?" she tested, across the void.

"Nell! Is it really you? Where are you?"

"In a cleft, overlooking the shaft. I have no light."

"Don't move an inch!" A tiny light went on, over to the right. "I see it on the map. It's a dead-end. I'll work my way around to you."

And so she waited. Happily. They'd won. After a time she heard his step. Craning her head, she saw through the cleft a pencil-thin ray of light. The light at the end of the tunnel.

She wriggled out of the little crawl-space and he helped her to her feet, smoothed back the wet hair, exclaimed over the bruised cheek, then turned out the little penlight that was attached to his keychain.

They held each other in the sweet darkness. Why was it so sweet, she wondered vaguely. He smelled of soap. Nell suddenly laughed.

"What's so funny?" he asked.

"Did Biz squirt you with the soap dispenser?"

"*What!* Is *that* what happened? After you came flying in and shone the torch at yourself and took off, some mad fiend came running out of the shadows spraying soap in the air."

177

For a few moments Nell was helpless in a spasm of laughter. Then she sobered. "It was Biz! Where is she now? She has no light."

"Probably back there, sensible woman, staying put!"

"If I'd stayed put, you'd be the one at the bottom of that pit, not Miles," countered Nell. "How did he manage to fall in?"

"When he went after you, he made the mistake of leaving his light on, so I was able to keep on his tail, wonky as I was," he replied. "He was ducking this way and that, zigging and zagging and doubling back. Then he stopped. He must have lost you. He seemed confused. He was cursing and searching around, as if he'd lost his bearing. He heard me coming up and turned out his light and began to run again. The blockade in front of the shaft was wide open and he ran right through it, and over the edge."

"Robin!" she cried, remembering. "He killed the pipefitter with that big wrench from the toolbox. He dragged him all the way from the main tunnel to the shaft, opened the barrier, and pushed him over. He was coming back for you when Biz and I got back here from the laboratory."

"The pipefitter! *Dead?* You really meant it when you said I'd be the one at the bottom of the pit! And how did you get so wet?"

Nell told him the incredible story of the flooded tunnel, of their swim out of the ultrapure, and of their climb up the cavity wall, all while the lab lay enshrouded in blackness.

"Incredible!" he said at length. "What a woman! I owe you my *life!*"

"And without you I'd have died by inches," she replied. "We're even!"

He chuckled. "We'd better head back now," and he produced a printout of the map she'd seen on the computer.

"Here we are," he said, pointing with the penlight. "We'll be out to the main tunnel in about ten minutes."

CHAPTER 22

When they arrived within sight of the main tunnel, the little penlight now at the end of its much conserved rope, the lights were back on. Biz, good woman that she was, had "stayed put", and though shivering with wet was none the worse for wear. Nell recounted the harrowing chase and the gruesome end for Miles.

"Where did you get the map?" asked Biz as they made their way back towards the lift.

"From Jack," answered Robin. "He knew it was Miles and was itching to go after him. But Carney, Washington, and Alex Wong had put their heads together and figured it was Suhara -- they were keeping him under close surveillance."

"I knew Washington suspected Jack," pondered Nell. "But why Alex Wong?"

"That's a mystery," replied Robin. "But Jack knew they'd never let him out of their sight so he passed me the map as we were leaving the lab."

Just then the tram came whipping around the bend and Bridges pulled up short, his worried frown fading to relief as he spotted the threesome. With him were two large RCMP officers and four miners with a load of rope and climbing gear.

Robin gave a brief account of the story to Bridges.

"Right!" said Bridges. "I'll get these boys down to the shaft to retrieve the bodies. You three get cleaned up -- the inspector'll be around to take your statements. There's to be a general meeting in the conference room when I get topside," and he rammed the trolley into gear and sped off down the tracks.

Nell stepped outside the warehouse into the late Sunday afternoon light. It was as if was emerging from a long dream. Life was real again; the hills were clear in the distance, the air was fresh, the birds still sang.

She returned to the trailer and examined her face in the mirror, gingerly touched the swollen cheek. It was bruised and painful but the bone seemed intact. Not too much to pay in view of all she'd been through. She showered and dressed, then walked over to the administration building to join the others.

As she entered the conference room, Robin, Jack Suhara and Alex Wong were intent on Morgan Washington, who was speaking in a quiet voice, his eyes fixed on Suhara.

"...so I have learned something very important today -- something I *thought* I already knew. I have judged a man, built up a case against him, and acted on that case. I was wrong the whole time. I misjudged you, Jack -- you did not deserve it in any way. I can't take back what happened, but I am sorry -- most profoundly sorry -- for doubting you. I see now that you have a deep commitment to this project and you surely deserve the respect and admiration of all your colleagues."

Suhara seemed embarrassed by this candid outpouring. He was composing himself to reply when Alex Wong spoke up.

"Jack, I would like to add my apology to Morgan's. When I was a child my father was killed during the Japanese invasion of China. We were very poor after that...my mother grew thin and died. All my life I have distrusted the Japanese people and hated their culture. I resented you right from the beginning of this project -- as much as if you had been part of that invading force that killed my father. I have been unfair it you, but now I want to put this behind us and work together as a team."

Jack was seated across the table from Alex Wong and Washington. He looked from one to the other, then down at the table. "Anyone can make a mistake," he said, "and I've made one that nearly cost the project."

"What was that?" asked Washington.

"I have suspected Dr. Oliver of sabotage for some time. I have watched him closely. On Friday night he drove the tram through the security doors and I knew then that we should change

180

the code. But it was the weekend and we had just started filling --
it was awkward to make the change because everyone using the
code had to be informed first. Well...I didn't get around to it. If I
had, the pipefitter would still be alive..." and his voice trailed off.

At this point Bridges came barreling in and took the chair at
the head of the table. Mintz and Hoff, Hilaire, Moira and
Hawthorpe follwed him in.

"Okay folks," began Bridges, "we've got a lot to get through.
As some of you've heard already, Oliver went berserk and tried to
wreck the lab. God knows why -- he's dead now and we'll never
know. He opened the bulkheads and half the ultrapure washed up
the tunnel. By some miracle the ropes held and the ball is in one
piece. Carney and Farraday are down there now, trying to crank
it back into position -- it looks like the damage is fairly minimal
but it'll set us back a week or two." He looked around at his
speechless colleagues, then resumed.

"The inspector will be here in half an hour to take statements
from everyone. We won't have all the details until later but I do
know that without Robin, Biz, and Nell here, things might have
been a lot worse," and he acknowledged them each with a nod.
"Nell, I believe you have the best handle on what happened down
there -- would you just give it to us in a nutshell please?"

"In ten words or less?" asked Nell, collecting her thoughts.
Leaving out her own role as ivestigator, she sketched just the
barest outline. How Dr. Oliver had jumped the trolley on its way
back to the lift and then entered the honeycomb; how the young
pipefitter had been killed giving chase; how Oliver had returned to
the lab to release the ultrapure. How he had gone back to the
honeycomb to drag the body to the mineshaft, then somehow
managed to fall in himself. She glanced at Robin: hand over his
mouth and eyes turned down, a trace of amusement showed
through. Yes, the story had been abbreviated almost beyond
recognition, but it would have to do for now -- even Siegel was
still out of the picture.

"How on earth did you *see* all this?" asked Moira in disbelief.

"Right," said Bridges, over-riding the question. "That shaft
goes down a long, long way. It used to be full of water. We
pumped it out to dump the tailings from the project excavation --
it's like a deep well now, half full of rock and water. We've got

four miners down there trying to bring up the bodies. Right. Now the press will be here as soon as the inspector is done, so we've got a full afternoon ahead of us..."

Siegel had not been able to reach Bridges during the time that the subterranean drama had played itself out. A Sunday afternoon, there had been no one in the office to take his calls, and the little cell phone in Nell's purse had rung countless times unanswered in her trailer room.

It was ringing once more as Nell and Robin slipped into her room to call Siegel before the questioning began. A frantic Siegel, sounding more like Bridges than himself, bellowed into the phone.

"At last! Where in God's name has everybody been?"

"Oh!" said Nell wearily. "You didn't get through to Mike?"

He'd been unable to reach anyone since he'd issued instructions to Robin, a couple of hours earlier, to get Nell off the project.

"And what, may I ask, are you doing there now, Mrs. O'Donovan?"

Nell and Robin took turns unveiling the afternoon's events. Amidst assurances that the ball was intact, they related the two deaths and the inevitable involvement of press and police.

"It couldn't be much worse," groaned Siegel.

Robin was on at the time. "Oh but it could! He would certainly have killed Biz. He would have had time to wreck that lab beyond repair. And he'd still be alive and playing the injured party. Siegel, you wouldn't *believe* the guile of the man! He was a monster!"

It was Nell's turn to pour oil on the waters. In time, Siegel was mollified. "All right, Mrs. O'Donovan, it looks like you've done a fine job for us. You'll probably want to be getting home. After you've given your statement to the police, feel free to pack you're bags. I'll be in touch with you over the next few days."

◆

Nell had never been happier than she was that Tuesday in November to walk up to the door of her own house. How sweet it was, this cold, rainy outdoor afternoon with the sea pounding on the sandstone. Home, back to the wildness of that isolated shore. Perhaps she would rig up the little tent for a spot of winter camping, immerse herself in the elements, wash away the traces of that dark unnatural dream...that November deep.

The telephone was ringing as she entered the house. "You must have had good connections!"

Her heart lightened even before she fully recognized the voice. "Smooth as clockwork," she laughed, "and only half an hour wait for the ferry."

"Just to wind things up," said Robin, "we found out more about Oliver. He was being blackmailed over that brothel incident in London. They reckon one of the boys in blue sold the information to finance a drug habit."

"Blackmail! How did that come to light?"

"His wife suspected something of the kind. When she learned of his death she went through his files, found the letters, and called the police. It was the second case involving the same officer. They're laying charges."

"So he was financially strapped," marvelled Nell. "That explains why he couldn't afford to be wrong about the neutrinos. But I thought it was more than that..."

"It was...a lot more. The psychiatrist released his files to the police. Siegel's faxed me a page, for our eyes only. Ready?"

Pelt was leaning his wet body into her best wool slacks. "Absolutely!"

"'This man has created an extraordinary identity. He has crafted himself into a work of perfection, and like Narcissus he watches himself as another might watch a garden grow. The supreme object of his own admiration is himself performing...'"

"Yes!" said Nell. "The way he lost himself in silverness..."

"There's more to come," said Robin. "'At school he was small for his age, highly intelligent, sensitive, and bullied about. Turning away from his peers he sought distinction through studies, moulding himself into a prodigy of erudition and knowledge. In short, he masked the painful child with a brilliant little adult.

"'The little adult grew to manhood, but the inner boy dwelt beneath the surface, with all his unresolved vulnerabilities and inflicted hurts. This psyche is split between the underlying boy and the powerful cultivated man that is shown to the world. The boy, still wishing to live and know himself better, is fascinated and drawn towards vulnerable young boys who resemble himself. But the man fears his old vulnerability and is caught in a conflict between loving and destroying the outer manifestations of his inner boy...'"

"That's *it!*" exclaimed Nell. "It accounts for how he treated that lovely Indonesian kid..."

"It does indeed! Nearly finished now," said Robin. "'He is drawn to the sensitivity and vulnerability of these boys, yet he must avoid the memory and emergence of the old pain in himself. He lives in this contradiction and as Jung put it so well, the inner reality must perforce act itself out as fate.'"

"It's uncanny," said Nell. "He doesn't seem like such a monster when you think of that little boy trying to get out..."

"Probably resembled the Indonesian lad..."

"But stunted and deformed, like a wind-buffeted tree."

"He wasn't a tree, though," said Robin slowly. "He was a man -- he had choice. His conflict killed the pipefitter too. Miles had no *courage.* He took the path of least resistance. Brilliant he may have been, but he didn't apply his intelligence to his own psyche -- he was void of wisdom, of responsibility. Failure to know himself spilled over his own boundaries to contaminate the world."

"Amen," said Nell. How clear he was.

"One more thing." He seemed to hesistate. "Were you afraid, when you thought it was me?"

A long-forgotten happiness stirred within her. "Mortified. I could hardly see straight while I thought it was you."

"Just the words I wanted to hear!"

184

EPILOGUE

The ribbon-cutting ceremony was delayed for three weeks. Some of the photomultiplier settings had been thrown out of whack by the torrent of water. When the neutrino counts began to come in they were somewhat elevated over the counts of other laboratories but were not sufficient to solve the solar neutrino problem. Dark matter remained at large. Evan Houston's game was met with a surge of controversy, but contrary to his mother's predictions it sold out everywhere. Morgan and Hilaire married and lived together in solid contentment. Siddhu Krishna set up a website on the physics of consciousness. Dr. Hernandez died in his sleep, a happy man. There was not a banana in the house.

Elizabeth with her nephew David.

Elizabeth Woodworth is a medical librarian who divides her time between Victoria, British Columbia, and Galiano Island. She has traveled in Europe, Asia, and America. She and her husband Claud are happiest outdoors - walking, cycling, and sailing. Elizabeth has written widely on conservation issues. *The November Deep* is her first novel.

ISBN 155212579-3

9 781552 125793